Holy Mary!
The Unappeasable Cowboys

Murray Ewan

This book is dedicated to my dog and friend, Bryn, despite the fact he cannot read.

"If the sun refused to shine, I would still be loving you."
- Robert Plant

Contents:

1: *The First Hits ~ 7*

2: *Holy Mary ~ 17*

3: *Rockriver Gentleman's Saloon ~ 23*

4: *Every Cloud ~ 35*

5: *Acquiescence ~ 49*

6: *Biting Rock ~ 61*

7: *Silverfish Ranch ~ 73*

8: *The Vulture ~ 81*

9: *Ellis 'The Savage' Wood ~ 89*

10: *The Sasquatch Hunt ~ 99*

11: *Henry ~ 113*

12: *A Motivator Calls ~ 119*

13: *Bad Luck ~ 127*

14: *The Peak ~ 135*

15: *Holier Than Thou ~ 145*

16: *Draw ~ 153*

17: *Dust To Dust ~ 163*

Introduction and acknowledgements:

About two years ago, I was struck with the intense urge to create something to leave behind; either a novel, or a loosely defined "novella." I like to think I have hit a happy medium with this first instalment in a story I plan to take further and continue. Despite the many barriers that unexpectedly appeared in my way, finally this book is published.

It is interesting to see what I'm able to do in a time of difficulty, and these last two years have been a perfect example. I have found peace in writing, and it is satisfying to be able to utilise my emotions in a creative way. I hope that you, a valued reader, can enjoy and appreciate the story that has grown to be very important to me: *Holy Mary! The Unappeasable Cowboys*, a twist on the classic western algorithm, by sprinkling in a little tragedy, religion, and family.

Before you turn the page, allow me to thank those who have contributed to this book. Thank you firstly, to my parents, for their ongoing support, including my mother's grammatical expertise being dedicated to this book's editing and spell checking. Thank you to my friends for their consistent interest and suggestions, namely my close friend and roommate, who has helped move this story along in passing discussion and by offering ideas, and who has kindly donated his name to a character in these pages. Furthermore, to anyone else who has been involved, however minor, you have played a big part in the writing process. You would be surprised how effective a simple "oh, you're writing a book?" has been in compelling me to finish, hopefully making you all proud.

So, without further ado, enjoy the antics of these unappeasable cowboys.

Self-published in 2024.

1: The First Hits

The middle of nowhere, The Wild West of California, April, 1880

This wasn't supposed to happen.

The thought kept humming through Wyatt's head, harmonising with the intense heat of the desert. With dehydration so intense, all senses became one. Sight, sound, taste, smell, and the feeling of dry dirt between his fingers all worked together as a desperate plea to stay alive.

This isn't how it was supposed to end.

The thought that had been on repeat for hours, finally changed. Blood dripped from his mouth and onto the dirt, whilst his arms and knees struggled to keep him up. His back felt the weight of the sun pounding through the open sky. He knew that if he could look up, he'd only see vast and empty desert. Shaking, he lowered himself closer to the ground, with his tongue out, inching closer to the small terracotta puddle he'd made in the dust. Blood is fluid, and fluid meant hydration.

Seconds from a minor victory, a swift kick to the jaw threw him quickly to the side, launching a tooth and its blood onto the unforgiving ground. It hurt, but laying on his side, he could finally see upwards again. And upwards, he saw the unmistakable shape of a man looking down on him.

Like a blinding halo, the sun shone from behind the violent man's head, and his silhouette was all Wyatt could see, doing a fairly favourable job of providing a morsel of shade.

"Are you starting to understand?" said the man, in his unique, strange, but still Californian accent, "I am not a man to be toyed with." Amongst the black silhouette of this man was his thick moustache, pristine hat, and antagonising smirk. His voice was antagonising too, too cultured for a real cowboy, so clearly a product of wealth.

"Please..." Blood formed around Wyatt's teeth as he spoke, although, his voice was dry, and it hurt to speak. "I can't pay yet, sir."

The man leaned in closer to Wyatt.

"Sir?" he chuckled, "you've known me long enough now to know that ain't gon' work, boy."

Wyatt tipped his head down, still curled up like the foetal positioned mess that he was, knowing that he'd made a fool of himself thinking pleasantries with this man would have given him any chance. Strength in the face of adversity was never Wyatt's forte, but he was running out of options. Gritting his bloody teeth, he looked up again at this man.

"Carter," he muttered. Upon daring to speak the man's name, hatred flooded Wyatt's head. For Wyatt, hatred for this man was a lot of things; envy, jealousy, guilt, and the list went on. Although he knew this *could* all be his own doing, any man would be in denial.

There was a brief silence, and another kick from Carter flew straight into his stomach. Wyatt was too far gone already to express any notable reaction to this kick. He just jolted, wheezed, and curled up a little more.

"That is *Mr* Carter to you, boy! I say, I suddenly have decided I enjoy the formalities!" Carter laughed, peeking behind him, encouraging his two goons to laugh too.

I can't win this.

Wyatt was a bag of nails, perhaps this was the reason he couldn't decide whether he was more upset about dying, or more upset about the jokes that were being made at his expense whilst dying. His eyelids began to falter.

"Wake him up," Carter's expression switched seemingly instantaneous to seriousness as he gestured for his sidekicks to act.

The two young men sprung to attention, and walked to the feet of Carter's horse, where a bucket of dirt and water had been left to fester. The two together, heaved and lifted the bucket, and waddled over to the sunburnt Wyatt that laid half asleep on the floor, the wool shawl that usually engulfed him, torn to shreds.

"One, two, three!" they chanted like a pair of idiots struggling to count, before dousing Wyatt in half a bucket of warm stink. Wyatt gasped and jolted up into a seated position, the movement sending a shooting pain throughout every bone. Eyes wide, he was back awake, and like a ravenous animal, snatched the bucket of filthy water and began to gulp straight from the bucket, with every smack he tasted its bitter stench.

"If your whore wife could see you now," Carter spat, "guzzlin' like a dang hoss." His disgusted expression showed a true dissatisfaction for the way that Wyatt was behaving. Wyatt looked exasperatedly up at him, now having come to his senses, thinking only about the water, and went back for more. He saw only the inside of the bucket, desperately trying to drink faster than his throat could handle, praying he didn't see the bucket's base.

The unnerving feeling of someone watching prompted Wyatt to slowly lower the bucket. Just as it left his lips, the bucket was unceremoniously kicked out of his hands, and Carter's smirking face came into focus just a foot away from his.

"Now listen, kid, I don't give two dings about the money you're owin'. You could be the most yellow-bellied bull's ass in the world, and I'd know you still ain't got the money, you know why you're *really* here, don't you?" Carter smiled at the more coherent Wyatt. Wyatt listened scared, yet intently. "Instead, in exchange for my mercy, you are going to suffer, until you tell me where my sister is," Carter's smirk was intimidating and intense, knowing that Wyatt would dig a deeper hole, with the guilty conscience that Carter's sister was long dead.

Confidently, Wyatt pushed through, "Then we will both die here," such a long sentence could barely come out. Carter's smile turned into a laugh.

"Son, I have spent so much time in these flatlands, I know all the lizards' names!" he bellowed, whilst his friends laughed behind him, "only one of us is dying here, boy. Now tell me where she is. I'd like you to know that we are presently doing this the *easy* way," Carter waltzed back to where three horses stood, removed the gun from his belt, and placed it on a horse's back.

"Good girl, Cassie," he whispered, as he reached into the horse's saddle, extracted a razor, and flicked it open on his walk back to Wyatt. Carter's smile had flipped, and the blood that rushed through his veins was now flooded with hate.

Does he know?

Wyatt was delirious, wondering if Carter's sister had anything to do with his own fate. His mind sunk back to her unfortunate demise, and the all-too-familiar guilt that came with it, always encouraging any comfort to quickly turn into trauma.

Carter reached into the inside of his blazer, to reveal one cigarette. He crouched and lifted the razor and cigarette parallel to Wyatt's eyes, staring with merciless intent. Wyatt felt unavoidable embarrassment, and softly nodded at the cigarette. With the sharp dryness of Carter's fingers on his lips, the cigarette was placed in his mouth. Carter struck a match, aided by the lack of wind, and lit the cigarette atop Wyatt's cracked tongue, coated in the blood that had dried quickly in the heat.

"Do you see what kind of man I can be?" Carter said softly, knowing that he had forced Wyatt to remember their first encounter. Wyatt's nerves started to calm as he took in the first breath of sweet nicotine. This was all that was missing, nicotine to match the newly somewhat hydrated Wyatt.

Whilst thinking of his response, Wyatt's eyes drifted behind Carter, to see a distant horse and cart passing across the desert within his eye-line.

Could this be it? My way out? A saviour?

"Well, I never," said Carter, noticing Wyatt's eyes long for this rescue, "*The* Wyatt Wilson praying that a stranger comes to his aid," he sniggered sarcastically, "they ain't coming, kid. See out here, there's only one goal; get to where you're going before your damn hoss, or your damn *self* dies!"

The distant horse and carriage came to an immediate stop.

It is, for sure.

From where Wyatt sat, a man the size of a mouse jumped off from the distant horse, stretched his hand across his forehead, and looked in their direction. Wyatt's hope was beginning to strengthen. Carter saw this, calmly sighed and walked back to his horse.

"I wouldn't be so sure, Wyatt," he said, "picture yourself on your way to where you're going, and you see a situation," Carter gripped the ivory handle of the gun that he'd placed on his horse's back, "ask yourself; would you be dumb enough to stop?"

Wyatt flinched, for Carter was fast, and spun, stretching his arm to shoot. A bang shattered the silence, and a crack echoed and whistled through the emptiness. The distant man flopped like a fish, without making a sound. Carter's arm remained stretched, with smoke pissing from the end of his brass-laden pistol. Wyatt was deprived of breath, and his eyes fixed on the hope that had now been thwarted in an instant. Wyatt didn't know where his own gun was, he just had an empty holster; surely it was on one of the horses.

Carter turned to face Wyatt.

"A necessary sacrifice," Carter said solemnly, "for man cannot thrive without the loss of others. Isn't that right, Wyatt?" and just like that, Wyatt's hope coldly shut down, and his mind once again turned to Carter's sister and the fate he'd given himself.

"Carter," Wyatt forced out, and begged, "I don't know where she is, please, I can find out for you, I swear, and the money-," Wyatt's words were smacked from his mouth. With one hard slap, he was back on the ground.

"What did I say?!" Carter shouted, with the anger of a thunderstorm, "I know that you cannot pay! Do not mention it again!" As Wyatt laid on the ground again, Carter lifted his boot, and stamped upon Wyatt's skull. A crack could be heard for miles. And again, crack. Crack. Blood began to spill from Wyatt's mouth. And again. Through each kick, Wyatt could see up, to see the pure rage and unfathomable hatred that glowed in Carter's eyes. Carter lifted his boot again, yet withheld, and stepped back.

"Wake him up," he said again. Carter's sidekick friends, as per usual instruction, began to move. The bucket was almost empty, but they proceeded to throw the rest on Wyatt's head with a minor splash. This time, the shower didn't do much for Wyatt. He was in an unchangeable state of half awake. *Brilliant,* Carter thought. He began to pace. Not much can be done about a man half awake, once the old water trick had been used twice already.

What Carter hadn't realised, was that Wyatt was still fully conscious, trapped in a shell, with just his senses and thoughts. Wyatt stared into the oncoming horizon as he laid. The sun, like the rays of God, pierced his eyes. The heat pushed him further into the ground, like a blanket made from rock. Farther than he'd seen over the flat land as of yet, Wyatt could see one tree. A tree in this wasteland, was like a sign. Life can prevail.

For what reason is that in my sight?

Forgetting the scenario he'd placed himself in completely, Wyatt's mind focused on the tree, it almost looked like a crucifix in the haze.

Tree, he thought. One simple tree, to distract a man from his pain. Life can prevail.

Tree, again. Suddenly, Wyatt was in a state of almost bliss. His mind from its tortured state, had briefly become at peace with its surroundings. The heat had become obsolete, and the empty desert finally preached beauty. Life can prevail.

"I'd like you to sit up," said Carter, harshly waking Wyatt from his nirvana, noticing that his eyes were open. Wyatt could feel his brain commanding his limbs to move, but with each effort, every muscle shied and failed him. Carter took a foot, and pushed Wyatt's torso to roll it. Wyatt's body flopped over onto its back, and flopped again like a rag-doll to the other side. The view had changed, and Wyatt was met with the distant shape of Biting Rock; cliff-like hills that could be seen from every ten miles out. It reminded Wyatt of home, reminding him he wasn't too far. The view of Biting Rock was the cornerstone of his town.

I'm nearly home, he thought.

"You like that, Wyatt?" Carter asked, he too staring intently at the jagged edges of Biting Rock. There was a brief moment of peace amongst the four as they gazed out to their landmark, knowing that despite their differences, they all shared the same love for their home, and the mighty Rock that towered above it, with its jagged but gentle slope on one side, and its sheer, intimidating cliff on the other.

"Let's go there," said Carter calmly, still staring, "I want to see the view of Rockriver from up there," he turned to the men by his horse, "what do you boys think?" he asked.

"But-," shocked by Carter's idea, the taller man could barely think of an opinion, "but the snakes?" he stammered concerned, "the Biting Rock Rattlesnake?" He said quietly, scared to speak its name. A snake, native only to Rockriver's monument, the Biting Rock Rattlesnake was a fairly peaceful creature. But its name echoed through the locals' folklore, and was always in the back of these cowboys' minds, as a fearsome killer, with a venom that kills painfully, in seconds.

"Billy, don't you get yellow on me, now. Don't bother the snakes and they don't care none," Carter retorted. Billy looked to his friend next to him, and both of them hesitated. Billy spoke again.

"H- how we gon' climb that?" he asked with uneducated drawl, this time with his hat in his hands.

"At the back there," Carter pointed, "I reckon a path leads up to the cliff, hell, how would so many folk die up there if they never got on it in the first place?" he chuckled. Certain, he briskly walked to his horse, placed one foot in her stirrup, and jumped atop. "We'll take the horses until it gets too steep, then we walk. You two grab the idiot," he said and pointed to Wyatt.

"You get the head, Al, I don't want no blood on my hands," said Billy, as he reached down for Wyatt's dusty boots. They heaved up Wyatt, and swung him over to the horses. Wyatt's body slapped onto Billy's horse, draping on each side. The view was less attractive now, just dirt and hooves. Billy hopped up to have his back to Wyatt. Al's horse was smaller, but no easier to mount.

"Everybody ready?" Carter looked back to see Al and Billy settled. "Wyatt, you ready?" There was no response, "good," he nodded, "Wyatt, this'll be a long journey, and I want you to take this time to consider where we are going, and why that might be. Reflect on what you have done. Perhaps on Biting Rock, you will decide to be more gracious," Carter turned back to face Biting Rock and smirked at its glory.

"Hyaa!" with a quick whip of the reigns, Carter was on his way, and the others began to move behind him.

Each step that the horse took, pounded Wyatt's chest. The journey to the peak of Biting Rock was underway, and this is how he'd experience it.

Biting Rock is the end.

This thought was more merciless than the last, he knew no one would come to save him up there. The snakes were a terror, but to Wyatt, they weren't even the worst of it, the Rock was intimidating. Closer to the sun, farther from water, farther from everything. There was no way off the Rock in his state.

Every thud of hooves was a metronome, that aided Wyatt's memory. With just the sight of the dirt on the ground speeding past him, he was ushered, almost hypnotised, into a state of self-reflection.

2: Holy Mary

The Wilson homestead, on the outskirts of Rockriver, West California, January, 1880

Wyatt stared his reflection down in the mirror as he perched on the edge of bed and began his morning like any other: looking around to ponder what he'd do with the house once he had more money. The walls of the room he slept in remained plain, with the exception of his mirror, and the prized photographs in its reflection: himself, his brother and late mother, placed next to a smaller portrait of his wife. He was a man who had a small number of possessions, keeping just the things that mattered most.

It was cold, more or less the middle of winter, and the urge to get back into bed was a little too tempting. However, Wyatt had a wife to greet, and a positive attitude to upkeep. Perhaps a little whiskey later on could dampen the weather's harshness.

He stood and shawled his poncho around his body. His jeans were folded on the floor. He knew Mary must've been up early to have laid them out, whilst his second pair dried on the line. He smiled. He strapped his cheap belt and gun around his waist. These days, every man, and many women, carried a gun, though some folks went their whole lives without ever using any of the six bullets. A force of habit for some, especially in Rockriver.

Wyatt considered himself lucky to own this house with its little kitchen. Walking inside, his smile stretched, as he saw the back of Mary standing over the cooker, the wooden cross hung on the wall just above her head. She turned to face him and her smile lit the room. Wyatt felt time stop every morning, every time he saw her dress flow when she turned, like a calm, warm breeze. Each endless curl in her hair twinkled in the morning sunlight streaming through the window.

"Good morning, my sweet. Overland trout?" She giggled. It was cute when she tried to use the same slang as Wyatt. Wyatt sat at the makeshift table fashioned from remaining planks of wood after Wyatt had built their home, and Mary laid a plate of bacon in front of him, sizzling. A welcoming smell for Wyatt, one of home. With her own plate, she sat opposite him.

"You use this eatin' iron, cowboy," she smiled, "especially if you're skippin' out the Lord's Prayer," she mocked, twirling a fork between her fingers before passing it to Wyatt.

"Holy Mary," he muttered affectionately, yet with a hint of mockery, as he took the fork from her hand, and began to eat.

"So, what's the plan?" Mary glimmered. Wyatt still focused on his food, barely noticing her speak.

"Oh, erm," he grasped at words, trying to let his brain catch up with the conversation, "work, I guess," he said half-heartedly.

"Borin'," Mary teased, taking a delicate bite so as to not smudge any carefully applied makeup. One of the things Wyatt loved about her, was the everlasting effort to impress him with her beauty, even if all she was doing that day was cooking, cleaning, gardening, and waiting for him to come home.

"Work and then spend some time with my favourite lady?" Wyatt smirked, trying to guess what she wanted.

"Hm," she smiled, "gettin' closer."

"I'll think of something," Wyatt said as his smile became a little more disinterested. He seemed distracted.

"Wyatt," Mary asked as her smile faded, concerned, "you okay?"

The extent of Wyatt's good mood slowly began to diminish further. His head sank, and Mary noticed. Then it hit her. 14th January.

"Oh, I know," she said softly, realising, "three years today?" she asked calmly. Wyatt nodded, picking at his bacon, eating small bites to keep his loss of appetite at bay, almost like a distraction.

"I just want to find him," said Wyatt, staring down at his food, "every year I think that."

"I'm sure he's out there somewhere, doin' fine, and livin' fine," Mary said with a forced smile.

Every day, Wyatt wished he'd go and find his brother, but every day, it was something that was too much to handle. Mary's hand reached over the table to meet Wyatt's, and she looked longingly at him.

"What do you always tell me?" she asked, her blue eyes gazing through his soul, trying to lighten the mood.

"I'm gon' buy us a ranch," Wyatt responded, aware of her needs over his.

"You're gon' buy us a ranch," she said reassuringly, "don't you worry about Joe right now, he's gon' be out there somewhere. Eat your breakfast, and get out there."

What Mary didn't know, is that Wyatt had lost his job at the paper mill a couple of weeks back, for fighting, and each morning he'd only pretend to work, knowing she trusts him, knowing it'd only upset her to know they were running out of funds. He struggled to look in Mary's eyes when he thought like this, worrying that maybe she wouldn't love him as much, if he struggled to make ends meet, and God forbid, struggled to deliver on his promise of their own ranch.

The bacon smelt good, but with every time he swallowed, it tasted of guilt, and stress. He could almost taste the price of the meat, making him near choke. It was like the sizzling was a whispering guilty conscience in his ears.

"I will find him, Mary," said Wyatt after a pause, "my brother is out there, and he ain't too dumb. Hell, he don't know much no more, but he sure as hell knows how to look after himself." Wyatt's opinion was thwarted by an awkward silence. Mary knew Wyatt's brother well, and knew, for sure, he was strong, but to look after himself? Maybe not. Again, she reassured him.

"For now, Wyatt, we need to think of ourselves," she smiled, sympathetic for Wyatt's feelings. "Once Joe's ready, I'm sure he will come back, but right now you have to just pray that he's made it by the time we have enough to buy that ranch. You can fetch him, and he can live here with us." Mary took her hand away from Wyatt and began eating. Wyatt knew she cared only for him, and this was what truly reassured him.

Maybe everything is okay for now. He smiled as a reflex, just looking at her. She couldn't have been more perfect. Suddenly it didn't seem so bad, and the thought of money looked up. The thought of Joe being a vulnerable younger brother, became more as though he were just a vulnerable young man.

"Holy Mary," the words automatically fell from his mouth again, though he was fully aware it was a nickname that frequently embarrassed her. "Whatever did I do to deserve you? To deserve the two of us?"

Joy overcame Wyatt, despite his estranged brother, and he noticed he was truly happy here. But perhaps that is the feeling of love for some.

Mary's eyes, innocently, looked intently into Wyatt's. Not so much as a word could describe her feelings as her smile gleamed.

"I love you too," she said confidently, and stood with both plates, and returned to the kitchen counter.

Buoyed by Holy Mary's love, Wyatt began to think this could be the day for something new. He knew he wasn't going anywhere productive on this day, being temporarily unemployed, and so decided it was a day for self-improvement. Three years since Joe ran. Perhaps the anniversary of his brother's disappearance was a day to just hope he was doing okay, and rejoice in his independence, instead of wallowing in his own sorrow.

He looked up at the corner of the ceiling, and saw a drop of water peeking through the seal. He stared as though it wasn't really happening. No one had the kind of money to fix everything up, and surely not him. With that on his mind, there wasn't much else to do other than continue to meet new people, and hope an opportunity came his way, before the paper inevitably ran out.

From the quickest gunslinger in Texas, to the slowest in California, he thought. Though not necessarily a bad thing, the thought was a little tough sometimes. He couldn't be the same man that he was in Texas. *That* Wyatt sinned, and *that* Wyatt didn't have Mary.

Wyatt looked down at his hand, instinctively flexing his fingers. He flinched at the stiffness, the wound he had sustained in Texas was a painful reminder of why he'd had to leave. It made his shooting less accurate, and his legacy less credible. Despite wanting to leave the past behind and trying to accept his damaged hand as a blessing in disguise, the large scar served as a constant reminder of the life of a lawless cowboy, how it can all go south, and how bad decisions can ripple into the future.

3: Rockriver Gentleman's Saloon

Central Rockriver, West California, 1880, minutes later

Hands cold, and legs moving, Wyatt only had to walk a short distance to get to where Mary thought was work. Despite the dark of the morning, Rockriver Gentleman's Saloon- or "Ida's", as the locals called it- was wide awake.

On a Tuesday morning, it was unlikely that Ida's would have much business. But as fate would have it, a dozen men sat lonesome amongst its impressive ground floor as Wyatt arrived. Every morning drunk surrounded by the familiar colour of oak. Quiet, yet welcoming for a Tuesday. Perhaps some of these men would greet him, shake his hand, maybe offer him some work. He hoped so, but saw that they all looked to be just drunken fools.

Strolling slowly towards the bar, he noted a few eyes following him with each step. The ceilings were high, and he could feel more eyes on the balcony that lined the interior too, even feeling judgement from the closed doors on the second floor. Ignoring the strangers, he placed his hat on the bar as he sat. Ida, with her scruffy hair tied high and grease on her gown, was stood behind the bar cleaning the last of last night's glasses. She admired Wyatt's eagerness to drink this early in the morning, with youthful hope for her business to thrive.

"They won't stop staring." she said, scrubbing a glass as she smirked at Wyatt. "Three years now, is that right?" she asked, putting the glass away and pouring Wyatt's usual glass of whiskey. Wyatt placed two bits on the counter and rubbed his head within his palm whilst he nodded. In his own little world of self-pity, he'd almost forgotten how infamous his brother was in this saloon.

"It's almost as if you've been counting the days too," sighed Wyatt. Ida scoffed with a smile whilst filling his glass up to the brim. She passed it to him and his hand wrapped around it with warmth. The first sip was hot, but loving. But the second felt the same as usual: just whiskey. The whiskey got him back to remembering Joe, and his infectious smile, youthful courage and arrogance, and his keen charm that levelled that arrogance out. The earlier memories of Joe were the ones that Wyatt was more fond of; Watching the teenage Joe becoming a stronger ranch hand as he helped Wyatt at the Silverfish Ranch back in Texas, teaching his little brother everything about how to make a good man of himself, crafting, survival, shooting, and other things Wyatt had picked up as the man of their old house. Of course, with the end of the war, came the harder times. Everyone in America dabbled in petty crime to help out at home. Wyatt and Joe would leave their home at night, and pick up a few bucks from whichever sorry sucker happened to be out. Despite Wyatt's best efforts to convince Joe that this wasn't what good men do, and that it was only a temporary necessity, he couldn't help but always think that a small part of Joe idolised the criminalised version of Wyatt, growing up seeing his older brother commit crime after crime, to pay for his mother's medicine. Perhaps this contributed to the day Joe left.

A sudden slam came from the balcony upstairs, making Wyatt shift to see a young woman storming down the stairs against the wall. A slightly older man quickly followed, fumbling down the steps, trying to retighten his belt around his waist as he hopped. It was hard to pinpoint his age, his fair skin said one thing, but his clothes and receding hairline said another. *Somewhere between 30 and 50,* Wyatt thought.

"Cassandra, wait!" the man yelled, with his hand reaching out causing his jeans to fall slightly further down again, his other hand attempting to hold them back up. The young lady snapped her body to face him and quickly pointed her finger in his face with fire in her eyes.

"Don't you speak to me again, Henry, I am *sick* of your lies!" she shrieked, holding back the tears.

"Sweetheart, come on," the man said softly to her, now aware of the entire building's population watching in awe. This was a welcome diversion in an otherwise dull morning. The balcony started to fill with the men and women that had been in the upstairs rooms. A sly slap knocked the man back, and he caught himself on his heels. There were quiet gasps that followed from those around. Wyatt noticed that she held herself proper, and reservedly, and approached this man closer, now with a tear that had managed to work its way out, slowly falling down her cheek.

"You take your pet names, and you give 'em right back to that *whore* upstairs," she said, choking on her words, "I swear, Henry, I made a promise to myself. If I *ever* caught you again, then I would leave your sorry ass!" She turned to face the door, and with her hands down beside her again, she left the saloon, crying, but physically composed. The man was left stood in the middle of the tables, hands on his hips, watching his happiness walk out the door.

"This town's full of assholes," said Wyatt as he turned away from the man in the middle of the room and back to Ida, now that the show was over.

"Takes one to know one," Ida said jokingly, bringing a small smile to Wyatt's face.

The embarrassed man walked lazily to the bar beside Wyatt. He too laid his hat beside his, and proceeded to sit and lay his head in his palm.

"Do you see the kind of man I can be?" asked the man, uncertain of whom specifically he was asking. Wyatt looked over, to question whether it was him the man was directing the question at. "I'm a mess," the man continued, with Wyatt now certain this conversation was headed his way,

"I'm sure there's a healthy explanation," said Wyatt, not sure of how helpful he could be.

"I'm a cheat of a man, sir," sighed the man, now directing his comments to Wyatt, who had unfortunately responded. "Hell, I see a girl, beautiful, and for five dollars, who am I to refuse?" The man's guilt was showing through each word he spoke, grasping at straws to find an excuse. "Hey, at least you've gotten a bit of fun to go with that whiskey!" He forced out a chuckle. Wyatt was more fascinated by the man's teeth, which were whiter than the average Rockriver man's.

"Yes, sir, that certainly was an interesting interaction," said Wyatt, staring at the man with anticipation. The man's nearly balding head, contrasted his thick handlebar moustache, which looked to Wyatt to be a remarkable upside down set of horns. The man leaned a little closer to Wyatt and pointed behind the bar to a wanted poster that had been on show for the past three years.

"Hell, I'd say I'm the most action this place has seen since that sorry sucker!" he exclaimed. Wyatt looked over at the picture of his brother that hung on the wall, with the words *Big Joe, Wanted dead or alive, $500 reward* framing the photograph. Wyatt refrained from mentioning anything about his brother to this stranger, and just went along with it in silence, thinking $500 was a shameful amount to place on his brother's head. "You're awfully quiet, sir," said the man, awaiting a response from Wyatt.

"I'm sorry, sir," Wyatt replied, "I'm used to being here on my lonesome," not intending to thwart incoming conversation, but awkward nonetheless. The man continued to talk, and pointed again at the poster.

"My little sister used to go on and on about that there Big Joe, every day it was *we're gonna be married, we're in love,* but we never believed her, and never once did I see her and Big Joe in the same room! Kids, huh?" The man began to monologue, and as he did, peaked Wyatt's interest, as although this man didn't believe in it, Wyatt used to get the same stories from Joe since moving to Rockriver the day Joe turned 18.

"Is your sister Miss Molly?" Wyatt interrupted, not considering it could make the man feel uncomfortable. But eerily, the man was taken aback by Wyatt's question, as though his mind had been read.

"…Y- yes she is, Molly is my sister," he said, a little stunned, "how do you-" he was quickly interrupted.

"Joe is my brother," said Wyatt excitedly, "and he was the same, always talking about Miss Molly, as inappropriate as that obsession was." The man watched Wyatt intently, and a smile grew slowly beneath his moustache.

"Well, by God! What a small town!" the man said as he slapped the bar and laughed. He had brought a smile to Wyatt's face at least. "So, that must make you the legendary Wyatt Wilson!" Wyatt scoffed a little at this notion, thinking back to old days.

"Henry, right?" Wyatt asked, changing the subject, remembering the woman's words.

"A perceptive man," the man chuckled, "Henry Carter," he reached out his hand to shake Wyatt's.

"Nice to meet you, Carter, I'm the legendary Wyatt Wilson," he laughed sarcastically, and shook Carter's hand, and it was clear to the two of them they were to get on.

"Nice scar," Carter pointed to Wyatt's hand on the bar, "so is that true? You can't shoot no more?"

"Well spotted," Wyatt chuckled, "I'm sure I can shoot if I had to," he smirked, saving face.

"Presumably, then," Carter continued more comfortably back to the topic at hand, "you are to tell me that those days are behind you?" he smiled. Wyatt joined in his smile, having his situation seem more lighthearted now that he could share it with another man.

"Yes, sir, I moved to Rockriver a changed man, and I'm a little concerned that you know of my past," he grinned, nervous that his past may have made its way to Rockriver, yet somewhat trusted Carter, so it seemed okay. For now.

"Oh, son, I'm just a sucker for a good story," Carter gestured his hands charismatically, "I love to yarn the hours away with long stories of any cowpokes, from any towns, and I am a *big* fan of the old tales of you and your brother, the man and his teen brother, not a man in Texas dare speak their names!" he quoted the old sayings, "I always wanted to meet the two of you, but this town grew bigger these last few years," Carter was correct. Since Wyatt and Joe moved to Rockriver four years ago, the town grew rapidly. Of course, this had its benefits, like meeting Mary in the first week, but it also had its downsides, like gossip spreading faster, and eventually reaching a stranger in a saloon, an unwelcome type of fame in Wyatt's opinion. Wyatt thought on this a little, and figured, he had nothing better to do, and entertained Carter's interest, feeling a glimmer of confidence in his newfound fame. He turned to Carter to become more involved.

"What would you like to know?" Wyatt asked, with a trusting smile on his face, ready to talk of the days that led him here. There wasn't anything particular about this man that trustworthy. But to Wyatt, he seemed to carry himself well, like a rich man. Maybe trusting him was a good route to employment, or a bail-out. Or maybe he trusted him because of the whiskey. Carter was clearly intrigued, the smile under his moustache grew.

"Tell me it all," said Carter, with enthusiasm in his voice, "how does a pair of renowned Texan bandits end up in Rockriver, only for one to lose his shit and disappear for good?" A little hurt by the way Carter had described his brother in this question, he passed it off as uneducated ignorance, and proceeded to tell his story.

"Well, Carter, the first thing you need to know is that I wouldn't call myself a bandit, we were ranchers. The last few years in Texas, my mother got sick, and me and *big* Joe did what we needed to do to pay for her medicine, seeing as our pops didn't leave shit for us, making us more *desperate* ranchers." Wyatt hesitated to call his brother big, but figured it was fitting for a fan. "Sure, we got in trouble, and in the end, there was a job that went south, and we had to run. Our mother was killed that day…" Wyatt slowed down, "the illness didn't even get to take her. California was far away from all the sourness, and especially the enemies that Joe and I had made, so we fixed to put the egos and sadness aside and say, what's the harm in runnin'?"

"But you didn't escape it, huh?" Carter prompted, "or what happened never would've happened." Carter was truly intrigued, almost showering Wyatt with affection. Carter could tell that this story meant a lot to Wyatt, and knew somehow that things had somewhat gone downhill since marriage, clearly seeing that Wyatt had settled for marriage and loved it, but also that part of him missed the good old days. Wyatt remembered how the 'Wanted' poster got where it was: that was a difficult night. He looked up again at the poster and frowned.

"That was one year after the day our momma passed on, one year after we ran from Texas," he said monotonously. "We actually did escape it all to an extent, but the day Mama died, Joe changed too, and as it happens, Joe didn't change too well." He remembered that fateful day, how Joe switched, from a promising young man to an unhinged and angry, suffering boy. Then came the one year anniversary. "It was almost as if…" Wyatt choked, "he just couldn't hack it, or somethin' went wrong inside him on that last job, I don't know, either way the child inside came out to cry…" His eyes sunk again, but he composed himself, remembering he was in the company of men.

"I hear that," said Carter, "I hear a lot of stories about Big Joe, the child in a man's body," he said solemnly, again quoting the old sayings. "Crazy to think, seven feet tall, and tiny on the inside. Does that sound about right?"

"He weren't always that way," Wyatt interrupted, "and seven feet tall? That's a stretch," he laughed, "he was only young, but he weren't too bad when we came here, and for the best part of the year, he was a good, honest young man, if not a little slow," he said as he tapped the table in rhythm. He thought a little, "Miss Molly would've been lucky had she kept him around."

The pair of them silently sat for a long moment, almost symmetrical. From Ida's point of view, she felt compelled and butted in.

"If you ask me," she said, waking the men from their daydreams, still wiping the glasses, "I think Big Joe's an ass after what he did here, sure, but every man has a few redeeming qualities, and it sounds like he had a bit of a thing for Miss Molly," teasing, changing the subject back to lightheartedness, she winked at Carter. Carter chuckled as the three of them wagged their chins.

"Well, go find him, Wyatt! Bring him back to Molly!" Carter joked. *Just kids*, he thought. Wyatt thought a little more seriously on this, as it was more genuine to him. He truly missed his brother, so much so that it hurt, he wanted him to come back more than anything, and run the dream ranch with him and Mary.

"Have giant idiot babies!" Ida continued, now hurting Wyatt, but he didn't let it show. But unable to control his emotions, he let it out.

"No wonder he smashed the shit outta this place," Wyatt said with a hiss, and stared at his drink in the awkward silence he'd created. Both Ida and Carter were stunned just a second, but thought it might be better to prolong the lighthearted mood.

"Wow!" Carter said sarcastically, "Lord save me, from the legendary Wyatt Wilson," he said, barely holding in his laugh. Ida's face became red holding in laughter, staring right at Carter.

"Yeah, yeah," Wyatt tried to divert them, the whiskey having an effect now, "you had your fun with Joe, come on," he said with a little smile.

"He's a freak," muttered Ida. Wyatt slammed his glass of the table as his smile dissipated, and the thud echoed in the self-made silence throughout the bar. Carter and Ida shared a look of concern, before Carter broke the tension.

"Sorry, pal. Just a bit of fun," Carter quieted down and went to place his hand on Wyatt's shoulder, but they both hesitated. Wyatt knew this was no time or place for any more worry. Slowly but surely though, the hand touched the shoulder, and peace was made. Carter truly felt moved, and although his face and words wouldn't show it, he was sorry for the comments that were made at Joe's expense.

Wyatt looked over the bar amongst the silence, and held his vision on the dents that Joe's fists had made three years ago, a year after their mother passed. He was too strong for his own good, and just a few blows to the bar almost smashed it to pieces, all because of the rising price of whiskey.

Time dragged on. The gentleman became more oblivious to their surroundings as more whiskey warmed their chests. Through the day, they bonded, amongst stories that could make Carter smile, and memories that made Wyatt's day. 6'o clock hit, and the bar soon began to fill. Wyatt on the other hand, had places to be.

Sober thoughts, echoed in his conscience, with the first thought of going home to Mary. He knew by now that she surely would be caught up in wondering where he is. But as far as Wyatt was concerned, he'd made a new friend.

As the saloon grew busier, neither man noticed as Mary sneaked in within the crowd, her eyes landing on Wyatt with a stranger at the bar, figuring that this must be his way to unwind after work. She approached him with intention of gleeful surprise, and tapped his shoulder. Wyatt spun and choked on a gulp of whiskey, panicking.

"M- Mary?" he sounded stupid, trying too hard to come across as innocent. The shock in his voice was unlike surprise, and Mary could tell. Her mood changed progressively, from intrigue to interrogation, with hesitation.

"What's going on, Wyatt?" she asked nervously, knowing something wasn't quite right. Carter, drunk as a bum, chimed in.

"Well he's been here all day, yammering on about how that giant Joe weren't always a *freak,*" he laughed, joined by the malicious laugh of Ida, and the more comfortable smirk of Wyatt. With eyebrows raised, Mary began to realise the scenario they were all in.

"All day?!" she questioned "Damn!" Wyatt was silent, but upon not receiving a response, Mary furrowed her brow and kicked his stool, nearly knocking him over. "All day?!" she asked louder than he'd heard in a long time. She reached out and grabbed his ear to drag him off the stool.

"Owww!" Wyatt moaned, but not trying to push or shrug her off, knowing he had an awkward conversation coming his way. Carter and Ida laughed as he was dragged away.

"In the doghouse now, boy!" Carter yelled with a drunk smile across the face as Wyatt was dragged through the doors. Drunk wasn't anything new to Wyatt, he knew he'd be fine within an hour or so, just in the moment was he drunk and embarrassed. He turned back to Carter one last time to shoot a look as if to say *"women, huh?"*

Outside the saloon, Mary let go of Wyatt, and encouraged him to walk home.

"We're going home, and you are gon' tell me what is going on," she said sternly. Wyatt stumbled and goofily gestured for them to both walk. The silence on their walk home was deadly, silence that made the town seem louder than it actually was, but each sound was just a distraction from the matter at hand.

4: Every Cloud

The Wilson homestead, on the outskirts of Rockriver, California, 1880, two hours later

The chickens had come home to roost, and Wyatt's chickens were miserable. At home, it was cold. The walls waited in anticipation for the impending truth, as the pair sat quietly at the same table as before. Through the dirty window, Wyatt could see the prairie, that once was peaceful, and was now spiteful.

"I'm sorry," said Wyatt, biting the bullet and breaking the silence. His eyes flickered up and down making sure Mary was looking, briefly meeting her deadly stare each time.

"Much obliged," she said sarcastically, with a dead-pan stare, and without a single movement. Wyatt figured it was about time to try and convince her of his innocence.

"You have to understand, Mary," he leant forward a little, sad, "I never meant to hurt you, I figured you'd be happier not knowing and in due time I would find another way to pay our way."

"I trust you, Wyatt," she replied, still with arms crossed, "but as soon as you lie to me, a little piece of that trust dies." Silence followed, but Wyatt couldn't think of a word to say, thinking whatever he'd say would be the wrong thing.

"Mary-," Wyatt was quickly interrupted with an unexpected outburst from his wife.

"I suggest you take your horse, ride down to that *damn* paper mill, open the door yourself and beg that *asshole boss* for your shitty job back, Wyatt!" she bellowed, breaking her crossed arms to point and wave. Her shouting silenced Wyatt again, for he knew his boss was a strict man with no care for the common man, and begging would surely just ruin any chance he may have had.

"Mary, please," he insisted. Mary struggled to keep her mouth shut, but knew honestly that this was her better policy and so allowed him to say his piece.

"We got enough money to be patient," began Wyatt. "If we are careful, we can go another few weeks and I can find something new, trust me." He finished talking, gazed at her, and silence filled the air again. Mary sat uncomfortably, and thought perhaps he was right. It always took some effort, but Mary could calm herself, and did.

"Best get to it then, and not be sittin' face down like a goddamn bum in a bar," she said with her mouth twisted in an angry sneer, holding back furious tears.

"I know, Mary, I'm sorry. Lies and laziness aside, we can work through this together now," Wyatt responded. The two of them managed to coax out a little love again, and though it required no words, they both were in agreement.

"So no money," Mary looked away, "no ranch?" she asked, visibly disheartened. Wyatt sighed internally.

"We're gettin' that damn ranch," Wyatt said sternly, denying his feelings.

"Bold of you to speak that way from the doghouse," Mary managed with a strained smile. Her sense of humour was a little sarcastic, and often out of place. Wyatt shared a smile and they remembered their end goal, and how they should work together to achieve it.

Before Wyatt and Mary could make true amends, a knock hit their door. They looked at each other wondering who'd be calling this late. Cautiously, Wyatt gestured for Mary to stay put and slowly approached the door. He stopped in his tracks as he heard the whinnies of multiple horses outside. He looked back at Mary, as if to say, *who the hell?* She responded with a similar look of confusion, eyes wide and her eyebrows trying to suppress them. The knock came again, shocking Wyatt back to face the door. Wyatt creaked the door open, and there, to Wyatt's surprise, stood Carter, wrapped in a fur coat for the cold, with two men standing behind him. Carter removed his hat and his all too familiar moustache emerged from the shade.

"Sorry to intrude," said Carter, though he didn't look sorry, "but I couldn't help but feel at fault." He smiled eerily. Wyatt looked behind Carter to look at the two stern-faced men at his back. Carter noticed, and jauntily he continued, "oh, where are my manners?" He gestured behind him, "This is Al, and Billy - they're friendly fellas but they ain't too bright," he said with a beaming smile, visibly offending Al and Billy.

Wyatt was suspicious of the entire situation, but felt confident in his home, and still somehow comforted by Carter's presence. Both Wyatt and Mary remained silent, in a tense sort of confusion. With no concern for the lack of response, Carter carried on, "may we enter?" he said calmly. Wyatt looked back at Mary for approval, and she hesitantly gave him a tiny nod.

"Of course, Carter," Wyatt said with a forced grin, "it's good to see you again," and he gestured for the three men to enter his home.

"Your home is very beautiful," Carter looked around the kitchen, where his eyes met the chairs around the table, and where Mary sat. "You must be the *Holy* Mary, ma'am," he smiled and reached out for her. She obliged and allowed Carter to lay a soft kiss on her hand, "Wyatt has told me all about you, my dear." Mary looked over at Wyatt and their telepathy continued, as if to say *only good things, I hope, and what the hell did you tell him?* She was immediately worried that Carter knew too much of Wyatt's past.

"What can we do you for, Sir?" Wyatt asked just trying to speed things along, whatever they may be.

"Don't call me Sir," Carter responded bluntly, leaving no room for debate, "I hope you don't mind me imposing, Wyatt, but as a man having met one of my most personal heroes, I feel I must do all I can to help," he monologued. "I am a straight-shootin' man, and I hope it does not offend either of you when I say it is clear to me that you could do with some help." He was clear and concise with his point, still smiling through his facial hair. Within each pause after he spoke, the sound of his pocket watch could be heard through the fabric of his waistcoat, ticking quietly.

"You're a perceptive man," Wyatt paraphrased, making Carter chuckle a little, "what can we do you for, Mr Carter?" he persisted.

"Fair enough," Carter sighed, and gestured towards his friends. "My colleagues and I currently run a business in this town, under wraps," he winked. "Yes, yes, I know I may come across as your average cowpoke out here," he said, making Wyatt give Mary a sarcastic look, "but I am in fact a man of philanthropy, and please, just call me Carter," he smiled. Mary felt the out of place urge to joke.

"A moustache and suit like that, you ain't foolin' no one, *cowpoke*," she smiled at Wyatt. Wyatt responded with a more concerned look, subtly lifting his eyebrows to try and shut her up.

"Right you are, ma'am," Carter raised his hands, "busted!" he laughed, appearing as part of the joke, looking behind him at his friends.

"Please sit down, boys, I'll make some coffee," Mary chimed in, but the two gentleman stood true without responding to Mary's offer. Only a little offended, Mary continued to make coffee regardless, but only handed a cup to Carter and Wyatt, before retiring to a chair in the corner of the room. Carter and Wyatt had become the centre of attention, sitting opposite each other at the table, with the others in the room almost positioned as an audience.

"What is it you want to help us with, Carter?" Wyatt got back to matter at hand.

"Anything and everything, son," Carter boomed, "I know a friendly man when I see one, you kept me entertained for hours, son, and you scratch my back, I'll scratch yours!" He laughed.

"So this business," Wyatt sat opposite Carter, expecting a lucky opportunity for work, "what have you got?"

"Let me show you," Carter stood abruptly and walked to the window, gesturing Wyatt to follow, which he did. Carter pointed to the distant neighbour of Wyatt's house. "See that house over the prairie, there?" he asked Wyatt.

"Sure, the Burton place," Wyatt confirmed, awaiting an explanation. Carter continued to look at the distant house once he started to provide his statement.

"Seamus Burton was in a tough spot if you remember last year," Carter started, Wyatt remembered how depressed Seamus Burton was, but despite being a neighbour, he mostly kept to himself, so Wyatt knew very little about the situation. "He was on the verge of losing his home, but thanks to me, he's still there, now in one of the only brick houses in Rockriver," Carter turned back to Wyatt and smiled glimmering with pride.

"What did you do?" Wyatt asked, still concerned, and waiting for Carter to get to the point.

"You don't remember?" Carter asked arrogantly, but Wyatt knew nothing of this. "Never mind, allow me to continue. I came to Burton and his wife, with a generous proposition," Carter's ideals started to become clearer to Wyatt and Mary. "I offered security to them both, and they returned the favour with affordable monthly instalments, providing me with a passive income. Mutually beneficial."

At this point, Wyatt was savvy to Carter's business, and became a little irritated by the idea.

"You're a loan shark," said Wyatt bluntly. He stared Carter down, yet inside he was a little shaken.

"I am offended," Carter clutched his heart, overzealously, and looked at Al and Billy to gain moral support. Wyatt looked at the guns strapped to the men's waists, and became more aware of the manipulation that was taking place. "But listen, Wyatt, help is help, your financial security is your silver lining in our arrangement. For me, it is being one step closer to a whole town made of my bricks, if you'll pardon the metaphor." Carter smiled through his teeth at

Wyatt, and the room became unsure of how friendly this conversation really was. Wyatt had the eerie feeling that hands were about to meet guns, and unsure of why this was, he prepared himself to remove his gun from its holster regardless. It was clear there was tension, but perhaps this was just embarrassment that had been mistaken.

"Our arrangement? I am beginning to think that our meeting at the bar may've just been bullshit up to this point," Wyatt frowned.

"Oh, come now, Wyatt," Carter scoffed, "we're friends!" he laughed, attempting to maintain his advantage. "Wyatt, the good it would do for me to help *the* Wyatt Wilson of all people, are you really the type of man to take that feeling away from me?" he asked, with an overly expressive face. Carter snapped his fingers and Al approached forward with his hand entering the inside of his coat. Wyatt's suspicions rose, and his hand approached his gun. Al stopped upon noticing, and Carter raised his hands, for Wyatt and Al to halt. Al's hand reached slower into his coat, and presented a folded piece of paper, and handed it to Carter. Carter opened the sheet and turned it to face Wyatt.

"$5,000," Carter pointed at the figure on the document, "all yours for your hardships, and your ranch." Wyatt was in disbelief, and Mary looked at Wyatt almost going into shock. "I'm sure you'd want to know the catch, as it were?" Wyatt stayed silent. This kind of money had to have some hard repercussions as a replacement for their •problems.

"You shin this money from me, and I do not care what you do with it. However, you will pay it back to me personally, week by week, at $35 per week, for the next four years, with interest of course. Seeing as I like you, Wyatt, I'll give you a few days after you take the money, to open your ranch before you begin repayments. There is but one condition; should you wish to open a ranch with this money, then you open your ranch *here* in California, within riding distance of Rockriver, so I can personally make sure that you prosper," Carter's smile was wide, "I may even have one in mind." He tapped the paper on the table, "all right here in the contract."

The pressure in the room became a little intense, the ticking coming from Carter's watch seeming louder. Wyatt could see Mary and how uncomfortable she felt, making him question his own greed. However, this money could solve everything, and with a successful ranch, the money would come easy to pay Carter back. Wyatt scanned the document in front of him, and floated over a section entitled 'recipient's benefits'. True to Carter's words, it highlighted $5,000, and a week's freedom. However, Wyatt spotted a third benefit listed, and this caught his eye.

"What's this?" Wyatt pointed at the third benefit on the page, the third point seeming more ambiguous.

"Good heavens, Wyatt, I almost forgot!" Carter spat. Al and Billy produced a silent giggle. Carter read, "*Sought after knowledge,* that says, Wyatt." Carter hadn't provided much of an explanation, just more intimidating ambiguity.

Mary had become increasingly frustrated in her worried state, and spoke up.

"Elaborate," Mary said with force from her chair behind Carter, with an idea of what it could be. Carter turned his smile to face her.

"Wow," he scoffed, "a little fire in your eyes there, Mary. Compose yourself, my dear."

Offended, but compliant, Mary laid back into silence again, for Carter to oblige. Wyatt was in discontent, now knowing Carter had found a hold on Mary, now more in control than he'd previously thought.

"Sought after knowledge that I believe you will be happy to discover, as I happen to know what you want the most, upon learning it directly from yourself, son," Carter continued, leaving a pause to tempt Wyatt and Mary into his trap.

"Three years today, correct?" Anticipation grew in the atmosphere, as Wyatt remembered the unlikely connection that Carter had with him. Wyatt realised in this moment the knowledge he needed the most, and thought surely Carter did not have the answers.

"How the hell do you know?" Wyatt asked, baffled as to why anyone knew anything about Joe's whereabouts, let alone a slippery stranger like Carter.

"I know many things, Wyatt, as I have said, I am a sucker for a good story, and I know a certain story that you may love to hear," Carter explained, almost teasing Wyatt. This was the real deal, aside from the money, there was only one thing Wyatt wanted more, and Carter had found Wyatt's soft spot.

"You know what you need to do," he said as he tapped the paper once more. Wyatt looked to Mary for much needed advice, but she only stared back speechless. She held her tongue, believing this was not her place anymore to advise. Whilst looking over to his wife, Wyatt lowered his hand again towards his thigh.

"And if'n I don't sign? How about I take that information from you?" Wyatt stared dead into Carter's eyes, his smile diminishing, still riled up by his prior domestic argument.

Carter's hand too lowered to his holster, and in synchronised movement, Al and Billy prepared themselves too. The ticking in Carter's pocket was amplified by the silence, almost like the seconds were speeding up.

"Think it through, Wyatt, you're outnumbered, kid, and you're a changed man, remember?" Carter muttered. Wyatt withheld, having made a fool of himself, and stretched out his palm to expect a pencil from Carter, since violence was no longer on the table.

"Good," said Carter as he reached into his pocket and revealed a shaving razor. Wyatt felt the deafening stare of his wife, and when he looked over to her, he knew this was not a decision that only he should make, and returned his hand to his side, not ready to sign.

To Wyatt's surprise, Carter pushed the razor into his own finger, and a drop of blood trickled down his hand. He turned the paper and pressed his bloody finger onto the bottom of the page. He turned the paper back to Wyatt and held the razor out to him. Wyatt took one last look at Mary, and hesitated, for she looked scared. Wyatt's conscience came into play. He knew that no matter how much he missed his brother, his wife was there for him now, and was more important than the past or his own selfish dreams. Wyatt refused the razor from Carter, and placed his hand on the paper to claim its ownership. Although Carter was persistent, he was smarter than to push clientele too far, and accepted compromise.

"Alright, sleep on it, you don't need my signature now for it's already there," said Carter, accepting that Wyatt was not going to sign on this day.

"When you need me, find me at the address on the page, and remember that brick house," he encouraged. "You let me do this favour for you, and soon, every house in Rockriver will be made of my bricks and iron," he smile confidently, reiterating his goals and gesturing with the razor.

Tucking the razor back into his coat, Carter stood to go toward the door. Just before leaving, he turned back, and spoke only with his eyes. Wyatt felt a chill run through his bones seeing a man look right into his soul, a man who knew what Wyatt needed, and knew who was in control. Carter turned back and swiftly walked back outdoors, with Al and Billy just two steps behind.

The paper remained on the table, like a beacon of hope for Wyatt, and a fearful gamble for Mary. Within the silence Carter had left them in, the sound of hooves began, and slowly became quieter, as their distance grew farther. The atmosphere began to settle, back to the way it was before Carter's visit. Wyatt looked to Mary for support, waiting for her to tell him to go for it.

"Don't," she said sternly, Wyatt could see she was unsettled. He looked down at the contract, hoping for it to turn into a miracle.

"We may need this," he replied, hope within his voice. Mary lost her temper, furious at the interaction that had just taken place.

"Are you kidding me, Wyatt?!" she shrieked as she stood. "What the hell does he mean by 'you're a changed man'? You told him all about your past, didn't you? And are you really this easy to control?" The fire behind her eyes grew, just as Carter had described.

"Mary, please, you're hysterical," said Wyatt, with instant regret.

"Hysterical?!" she yelled, "now look what you done, Wyatt!" she paced the room back and forth, seething with rage, until she stopped and pointed at his face. "When you came to me, you said never to tell no one, and that you trusted me to keep that secret, in case it caused a problem, and now here we are!" she chuckled, a sense of their misfortune almost becoming a joke. "You blurt out all the things you don't want folk to know about your past, and trouble comes knocking on our door!"

Wyatt knew his drunk conversations weren't a good idea, but felt the smartest thing to do would be to try and ease Mary's mind.

"Mary, I'm sorry, he already knew about me and I had a few-" he was quickly interrupted.

"A few, yeah, a few!" Mary said forcefully, "it's always the same with you, Wyatt, there's always an excuse! Nothing's ever your fault! Do you think we can get out of this one? He's got you by the *balls*, Wyatt!"

And there it was, another argument had started. Wyatt was quick to defend himself each time his wife's emotions got the better of him. Mary was scared, and this was apparent through her behaviour. Wyatt, on the other hand, was confident, that a deal with Carter could save his little family.

Mary came to her conclusion after a long while, and was unwilling to accept compromise.

"You will not take that money and leave us with any more trouble, Wyatt," she said with strict instruction, "and lie to me again, and there will be consequences."

Wyatt understood, and hesitated to question her authority. He loved her, and he wanted the best for her, and perhaps this was why a small part of him wanted to accept Carter's proposal even still. Wyatt knew that if he didn't accept the money, they'd still be in trouble, he had neither the heart nor the courage to tell Mary how little of their money was left. And overwhelming his already troubled feelings, was the thought of Joe, and how finally he could have a lead.

Wyatt was not an especially clever man, but a somewhat religious man. And with the cross that hung upon their wall, he felt protected amongst his family. Wyatt was consistently tortured by his indecisive nature, over whether life was better with Joe, or with Mary. The deal that Carter had proposed gave him a glimmer of hope of having both, the catch of course being in a man's debt. Although within that hope, being indebted to Carter was a small price to pay. And that's when it hit him.

"Mary," he spoke up. Mary had gone quiet in the last handful of moments, and was exasperated to hear Wyatt's voice. She paid attention to him again, as respect still remained active between them both.

"I miss my brother," he said, begging for her to understand. A glimmer of sympathy came through, but Mary was an intelligent person, and knew that no matter what the reason, no good could come from Carter.

"I have an idea," he continued, carefully, as though he were trying to tame an animal, "if you'll hear me out." Apathetic, she gestured for him to tell her his idea, rolling her eyes.

"It starts like this; I take Carter's deal, and I leave the money with you," he began. Mary sighed but Wyatt soldiered on. "Immediately, I head out to find Joe -," he said, but Mary interrupted Wyatt.

"What if it's a lie, Wyatt? What if this *stranger* doesn't know a thing? I wouldn't be surprised if you came out of this with a story of *El Dorado!* Then what?" she crossed her arms waiting for him to retort. Wyatt was stumped by this, but desperate men tend to gamble.

"We got risks, Mary, every day does," he grasped at straws, losing Mary's interest. Ignoring her point, he continued, "when me and Joe was on our way here from Texas, we rode through Arizona," he began to explain, "and there was little towns dropped in here and there, in between great horizons of land, grass was growin', trees were everywhere, and water was flowing through almost every town," he said excitedly.

Mary's sincerity was shaky, now knowing exactly what Wyatt was thinking, "Carter said it has to be here," her eyes staring, waiting for Wyatt to confirm his intentions.

"He said we have one month, if I can get Joe within a few days, we can be on our way to Arizona within two weeks, tops," he smiled trying to coax a response from Mary. She was hesitant and couldn't give her devotion to this kind of trickery.

"Don't you see we won't *have* to stay here? We could just run!" Wyatt's enthusiasm was convincing to an extent. Mary's thoughts floated around danger, but also opportunity. How many opportunities did people get in Rockriver? However, Mary's priority was safety now, not betraying strangers and disappearing only for *Wanted!* posters to appear.

"I thought those days were behind us," said Mary, skeptically, worried that a new found knowledge of Joe could change Wyatt back into a man she felt scared to love.

"We're a team, Wyatt," she reached out for his hands, and sat opposite him, "Wyatt and Mary Wilson, Wyatt Wilson from Rockriver, California, I'm not sure I wanna see the Wyatt Wilson you used to be," Mary held back a tear, yearning for the man she fell in love with to fight his urge to break the law.

"Mary, listen, one month and he won't know what hit him," Wyatt leaned forward and clutched Mary's hands in his, "trust me," he said sincerely.

Mary's tear had fought through, and she began to cry. She stood and wiped her tears, only to turn back to Wyatt to speak, her eyes had become red with sadness, and sick of Wyatt's relentless proposition, she begged him.

"Don't you break my heart, cowboy!" she pointed to him with tears streaming down her face, unable to contain her feelings, "I beg you, Wyatt, stay here, we can find a way, we can find Joe ourselves. I *want you to stay,*" she sobbed as she gestured in time with her words, terrified by the idea of her perfect life changing. Wyatt watched as his wife slumped into her chair again, the sound of weeping muffled by her face buried in her hands. It became apparent now to Wyatt, that there was no way he could get Mary to understand. Reluctantly, he told her that he would stay, and assured her that the old Wyatt Wilson was gone.

5: Acquiescence

Horse Livery, Rockriver, California, 1880, midnight

Stood wrapped in his coat with the livery towering over him, Wyatt looked down at the contract in his hand. He thought it was peculiar that Carter had listed the town livery as the relevant address. At least sneaking out of bed at midnight meant Wyatt could see his horse, whom he seldom got to spend time with, as travelling long distances had become less essential since he settled in Rockriver. The livery wasn't too far from Wyatt and Mary's home; it was walking distance. And most people in Rockriver, or on the outskirts of Rockriver, could keep their horses safe in the livery and simply walk to and from the stables.

The livery seemed to be the only place in town with a light coming from inside. It encouraged feelings of warmth, and coaxed him inside, as if to say that the livery was where he should be. Wyatt looked behind him to see the town, confirming that it was in fact asleep. The livery faced directly down the straight road at the heart of Rockriver, and its light reminded Wyatt of the star upon a tree.

He gently eased open the stable door, and peeked in. Sure, there were plenty of horses, but Wyatt couldn't see Carter. He opened the door wider, to see a man in a darkened corner of the livery, gently brushing a black horse and whispering incoherent words to either himself or the horse. The man's spectacles were so dirty that they were opaque.

"Carter?" Wyatt's voice echoed in the stable, breaking the midnight silence. The silhouetted man in the corner turned to face Wyatt, stopped muttering, and making no sound, retired to behind a wooden panel that separated the horses. A slight murmuring could be heard from behind the partition, almost like conversation, Wyatt tried to hear what was taking place, already unnerved, but the murmur was too quiet.

Wyatt gently and slowly walked through the stable closer to the partition. The sound of his feet pressing against the hay on the floor as he walked was louder than the murmur, so he knew his presence was known. Bringing Wyatt to a stop, another man appeared from behind the panels.

"Wyatt!" It was Carter. "Please forgive my friend, Floyd," he said, gesturing at the man from before, who snuck back out and over to the black horse in the corner to continue brushing it. "He's not an especially confident man," Carter continued.

Wyatt approached Carter in the darkened corner of the stable. "Is everything okay?" he asked quietly, put off by the rather bizarre encounter.

"Of course, son," Carter smiled and removed his gloves, "I'm glad you came, you feelin' hungry?" Carter pointed at a small table placed in a stall that a horse would usually stay in, with a large silver pot steaming atop.

"It's midnight…" Wyatt said slowly, "why are you eating at midnight?" Carter's smile became a little more forced.

"Well, I knew you'd come late, of course," Carter muttered quietly, but loud enough to hear over the sound of near nothing, "it's sofky, do you want some?" he pointed again to the pot. Wyatt waved his hand to decline, and walked over to greet Carter properly. Carter pulled a chair from behind the little table, and placed it at Wyatt's feet. When Wyatt sat down and placed his hat, Carter remained stood.

"I hope you don't mind if I stand," he leaned into Wyatt's ear and whispered, "I'd just like to keep an eye on Floyd." He winked at Wyatt and stood back upright to look over to Floyd, who was still eerily whispering to the horse he was brushing.

Wyatt looked around, "do you work here?" he asked, confused. Carter was not the type that Wyatt had expected to be working in a livery, he wasn't the owner, but there was no one else there.

"A man has to keep busy," said Carter, stirring the pot of sofky, "and if you can get a man's horse on side, you can get a man on side," he jokingly continued. Wyatt looked around for his horse, having not seen him in a while, and noticed him in a stall on the other side of the stable; short and brown.

"Do you mind?" he asked Carter once it'd become apparent that the horse he stared at was Wyatt's, as if to say 'please excuse me for one moment.'

Carter stopped stirring to grin. "Banjo is yours?" he asked. "Come on," Carter led Wyatt over to Banjo. Wyatt followed skeptically, thinking it strange that he wasn't just walking over to his horse alone. Carter opened the stall and proceeded to stroke the neck of Wyatt's horse. Banjo leant in to Carter and huffed.

"You mind?" Wyatt asked Carter again, more forcefully upon learning that his own horse was friendly with Carter. Carter backed off and walked away from the stall, saying nothing. He just smiled back to Wyatt and allowed some time between the two of them, knowing he'd maybe coaxed some jealousy from Wyatt.

Wyatt pulled an apple he'd taken from home from his pocket, and fed Banjo. There were a few things that kept Wyatt on the straight and narrow, but seeing his horse always encouraged memories of years passed, riding with his brother. Banjo, Wyatt reflected, was always a big part of his escapades in Texas, almost like another brother and part of the gang.

Despite fond memories, Wyatt couldn't smile at Banjo, because if the old days were to make a reappearance, he'd surely have gone against his wife's wishes. At the present moment, Banjo became a minor distraction from Wyatt's reasoning for where he was, like a best friend whose mere presence is a happy place.

"I'll be back," Wyatt whispered quietly to Banjo, and winked as he backed out of the stall and locked it up. Just one minute with his horse had been enough to boost Wyatt's confidence in his own plan. However, jealousy is a powerful emotion.

"I've grown quite fond of that'n," Carter said with a mouthful of food, when Wyatt was walking back over to him. Wyatt did not respond immediately, more annoyed by the idea of Carter getting a hold on Banjo.

"Back off my horse," Wyatt said with a deep tone, refusing to sit. Carter paused before he could take another bite of his meal, placing the spoon back in the bowl. He approached Wyatt to meet his displeased expression, just inches away, matching with stern silence, then fed up, broke the tension and sighed.

"Come on, Wyatt, it's midnight." Carter rolled his eyes, less intimidated than Wyatt had hoped. Before Carter could walk away, Wyatt stepped a little more forward, not breaking his eye contact. Carter looked back at Wyatt and let out a snigger, struggling to take Wyatt seriously.

"Something funny?" Wyatt muttered to Carter. Carter stared back into Wyatt's eyes and heard the slow sound of a gun cocking. Carter looked down to see Wyatt's hand on the pistol by his side. Carter rolled his eyes again, and laughed.

"I thought you came here for money! You gonna kill me for being friendly with your hoss, Wyatt?" he laughed as he backed away. Wyatt was left a little struck, Carter was right. "I suppose you'll have to kill Floyd too!" Carter continued laughing as he pointed to the darkened corner where Floyd had been.

Wyatt had all but forgotten there was another man here. Looking back over, Floyd, a silhouette still in a darkened corner, had stopped brushing the horse and was now just staring intently at Wyatt and Carter.

"Don't go hurtin' Mr Carter, now," came from across the stables, with a faint echo in the hush. Wyatt continued to look at Floyd, wondering what the reason was for this defense. Carter turned to face Wyatt again after shooting a smile over to Floyd. Between each sentence any one of the men let out, the silence was deafening, and Wyatt could hear his own heart beating.

"You ain't gonna shoot me, son," Carter sniggered, "I've known you two days and you've done that but three times," he laughed, and a small laugh echoed from Floyd too. Quiet followed, and the all too familiar ticking from Carter's pocket became prominent again. The three men stood apart, Floyd farther than the others. As the ticking got louder, Wyatt's thinking became more erratic, and he wondered if he should save face, or track back to the reason he came.

With Wyatt unable to make a decision, Floyd began to move, catching Carter and Wyatt's eyes as he walked briskly with purpose through the hay towards Wyatt, arms tensed and with a face like thunder. With once quick hesitation, in fear, Wyatt looked at Carter for a split second to see him sat down, smiling and entertained, and looked back to see Floyd nearing closer. Wyatt began to sweat - was this man about to attack him? As he neared even closer, Floyd reached down by his waist to draw a weapon, and Wyatt's instincts kicked in. Wyatt drew his gun in time with Floyd, pointing it straight at him, and pulled the trigger watching as Floyd dropped to the floor, just a couple feet away, with a hole in his head. The gunshot shook the wooden walls of the livery, and all the horses jittered, startled by the bang.

Wyatt stood dazed, still with his gun in hand. He hadn't aimed for the head, but he was out of practice, interestingly able to hit a target as small as a head, when aiming for a torso. With eyes wide, sweating and breathing heavily, he stared down at the mess he'd created, scared of the man he truly was. Shaking, he slowly turned his head to face Carter, who was still smiling, also staring at Floyd's bloodied body on the floor.

"Well," Carter broke the silence, "I'd say we have about 5 minutes before the town comes a knockin' the doors." He slapped his thighs and stood up, pulled his razor from his pocket, handing it to Wyatt with a wide grin, sparing no time.

Wyatt's heart was still racing. It had been a while, and his adrenaline had gotten the better of him. Uncontrollably shaking, but self-aware, Wyatt lowered his pistol back into its holster, still hot. Carter waited contently for Wyatt to take the razor from his hand.

"We really ain't got all night," Carter grinned, "I make that 4 minutes now," and he encouraged Wyatt to make a move.

Reluctantly, Wyatt reached out for the razor and approached the table. He was unnerved by how quickly they'd both moved on, but tried not to look back. Before Wyatt had a chance to think, a voice came from outside.

"Mr Carter?" came a muffled voice from the other side of the doors. Carter let out a small sigh, and a smaller tut.

"No minutes," he said snidely to Wyatt, and stepped over Floyd's body waltzing to the doors and leaving Wyatt alone at the table.

Considering the situation, Wyatt mulled over the thought of running now and forgetting the whole ordeal, but felt safest staying hidden behind the partition at the table. A quiet exchange could be heard from the doors. Peeking out, Wyatt could see Carter had only slightly opened the door, his face pushed through the gap, whilst he spoke quiet words with the voice from outside. After a short exchange, only a farewell could be heard, and Carter closed the door and walked briskly back to Wyatt.

"He may come back," said Carter as he looked back at the door, "we should finish up."

"Shouldn't we…?" Wyatt was confused and pointed at Floyd.

"Oh," Carter said, "don't worry about him, Sheriff owes me." He winked at Wyatt. "Now sign, before he comes back to find you still here." Carter smiled but it quickly faded back to a strict expression.

Wyatt laid out the contract on the table, but hesitating, he could not bring himself to sign.

"I have to let you know," Wyatt spoke to bring himself some ease, "this is for Joe."

"Of course," Carter replied.

"So I need to know you ain't playin' games", Wyatt looked needfully at Carter.

"I'm serious, Wyatt," Carter grinned, "I want to help you, as promised."

"And Joe?" Wyatt encouraged, "you can tell me where he is?"

"I can help," Carter finished.

Wyatt could feel his heart pounding, and blood filled every vein as he gripped the razor in his hand. With his thoughts torn between Joe and Mary, he lifted his finger, and slowly approached it with the blade. Feeling somewhat gullible, but also optimistic, he pressed the blade firmly and sliced into his fingertip. With each nerve that the razor passed, the battle in his brain raged on. Finally, with a press to the page, Wyatt had signed his rights away.

"Yessir!" Carter bellowed, snatching the contract from the table to hold it in the air, his smile wide and exuberant. Wyatt wrapped his bloodied finger in his sleeve, and watched as Carter tucked the contract back into his coat, completing its journey. "Now as promised," he said. Carter's hand returned to light from the inside of his coat, this time with a wad of cash waving in front of him. Wyatt's eyes widened, having not seen money stacked thicker than a pancake for years. Like a child, he reached out to Carter, and took the money from his hand. He gazed for a little at the stack of confederate dollars in his hand, in crisp fifties. Bewildered, Wyatt quickly stuffed his money into his pocket and stood. He revealed a pencil and a small piece of paper and held it out to Carter.

"Spill," Wyatt forced, as he kept his arms held true to Carter. Carter declined Wyatt's offer for paper and slowly began to pace around to Floyd's body. *Great, story time,* Wyatt thought, as he prepared himself to take notes on his own. Carter stood at Floyd's head staring down, with arms rested behind his back. Looking back at Wyatt, he smiled.

"One of my favourites," Carter started. Wyatt let out a little sigh, but was ready and anticipating the reveal. "My father owned the brewery up past the woods, north of Meller Creek," Carter explained, "you know the place?"

"I do, I used to see the woods on long walks," Wyatt responded, intrigued. Carter approached Wyatt to become a little more personal, stepping over Floyd's body as he walked.

"Now, after all working hard up there, the men like to hunt. Some nights they go into the forest, and they look for rabbits, squirrels, whatever's easy for a quick sense of achievement." Carter's story didn't sound at this point, like anything important, but Wyatt continued to listen. "However, any man would be scared if they came across a *monster*, right?" He waited for Wyatt's agreement, and only continued once Wyatt had nodded. "One man told another, that he swore he saw a *terrible monster* one night, and since then, that particular man never joined them on their hunts. They call it the *Sasquatch*. It was only once another man told a similar story, that all the men who never seen it, became obsessed with catching the beast." Carter was invested in his story, and so was Wyatt, despite it not appearing to be relevant.

"I ain't lookin' for no made up animal," said Wyatt, quietly, predicting what Carter may say next.

"That's where it gets interesting, Wyatt," Carter continued, with Wyatt's attention on his side. "That second man didn't describe no monster. Why, he swore he saw a *wild man*, seven feet tall, wearing the *skin* of a bear, and the wild man roared like a beast, scaring him forever out of the woods." The stables were now silent, processing a little confusion over a man that roared.

"He roared?" Wyatt asked, as his interest cracked a little.

Carter shrugged, "of course, that's just a story, passed around from man to man." Carter responded as his movements became more typical, "but if you ask me, a seven foot man? Why, there's only one for miles, son."

"The woods is a big place," said Wyatt, a little disappointed by what seemed to be a lack of information, and similarly just an old wives' tale. He held his pocket where the money was, trying to justify what he had done. Carter came a little closer to Wyatt, nearing his face, and spoke quieter.

"They talk of a group of old fallen trees, where it looks like the sticks and twigs have been fashioned into a group of shoddy shelters," Carter smiled, "about half a mile into the woods, must be where the *Sasquatch* is." He chuckled and backed off from Wyatt's personal space.

Wyatt couldn't picture his brother making shelters in the wild, but this information seemed to be as much as he'd get, so chose to believe it. He started to internally debate on whether he should tell Mary, or just head for the woods right after leaving the livery. He knew at some point she'd have to find out, or from a certain point of view, better late than never.

"I'm gonna go now," Wyatt said after a lengthy thought process, that Carter had patiently waited through.

"Well, you wouldn't want Mary to stop you," Carter winked, crossing his arms, and reclining into a chair by the table. He gave a small, belittling wave as Wyatt patted down his coat to leave, visibly trying to control his breathing. Wyatt nodded and headed for Banjo.

Mounted upon his horse, Wyatt straightened his hat, and looked to the doors.

"Care to get the door?" Wyatt said to Carter, as he rode slowly alongside him toward the exit. Carter nodded and led Wyatt to the doors, swinging one open with one heave, allowing Wyatt to pass. Just as Wyatt passed the door into the night, Carter called out one more time from the open doors.

"Oh and Wyatt!" Carter hollered. Wyatt halted Banjo, and looked back at the man who newly owned his freedom, whose smile was as prominent as ever. "If you cross me, and burn the breeze," he said, suspending his words, "I'd hate for you get awful sick," - his smile vanished - "from a bullet in your chest." Carter left a little time for a response before rounding off his farewell, "but, maybe Joe and

Molly could live happily ever after come the dawn," his smile returned, reminding Wyatt of their long saloon conversations.

Shaken by the thought of a twisted brother-in-law, Wyatt just nodded, and turned into the night, money in his pocket, and a difficult mix of betrayal and salvation on his mind. He whipped the reigns, took a left, and headed for the woods north of Meller Creek.

6: Biting Rock

Biting Rock, West California, April, 1880

Deep within the twisting paths that constructed Biting Rock, Carter led an effort to reach the peak, closely followed by his cronies, and Wyatt sprawled over a horse's rear. Carter halted ahead of them, listening intently to his surroundings. Bushes and shrubs were scarce at this section of their journey, and the surrounding canyon had few hiding places. It had been several hours, and it had gotten a little late as the sun was starting to set. The heat was beginning to mellow, and Carter turned to face his followers.

"You hear that?" Carter asked indirectly, as he smiled at the narrow canyon around him. Billy and Al both as confused as each other, tried to focus too on whatever it was that Carter heard, though couldn't notice a sound.

"No?" Billy asked, shrugging at Al whilst he spoke.

"Exactly, no snakes," Carter smiled. He jumped from his horse, gently stroked her neck, and spoke directly to her.

"Get some rest, Cassie," he said softly, before he pulled a saddle bag from of her back, and dropped it around 6 feet away from her.

Up until this moment, they had been followed by the threatening sound of rattles coming from the sides of the paths they chose. Al and Billy had been able to figure out that Carter intended for them to sleep, now that the snakes were either absent, or idle.

"Did you clean the pot, like I asked?" Carter asked, watching Billy and Al drag Wyatt off the horse with great difficulty.

"Yessir," said Al, leaving Billy to do most of the work. They dragged Wyatt's body by the feet over to where Carter had sat on the ground, whilst Wyatt began to wake and slowly shift his head.

"Good, because we're making coffee for Wyatt, but it'll be cold," Carter proclaimed, reaching his arm out, opening his palm for Al to pass him the ingredients. Neither Al nor Billy tended to question Carter too often, so they simply handed him the coffee and pot, and made an effort to sit Wyatt up as he steadily regained consciousness.

Where the hell?

He was beginning to wake back up. Every bone in his body was in pain, even immobile. Maybe some broken ribs. Face swollen all to hell. He managed to just about open his eyes, painful as it was, and saw Carter staring back at him. The light wind began blowing through Wyatt's hair, something he didn't tend to usually feel.

"You shouldn't touch another man's hat," the tiniest voice wheezed from Wyatt, only just coherent.

"Well look who's woken up," Carter said boisterously, stirring cold coffee. "No one touched your precious hat."

Wanting to join in, the others spoke up.

"Must've fell off your head when we beat your ass in the brewery," Al laughed, nudging Billy mockingly. Carter shot a look of disapproval over at them both, silencing them.

Carter passed cold coffee to Wyatt. It was unclear to Wyatt whether there was a plan at hand, or if there even was a plan. Maybe it was just that; coffee. Although it hurt intensely to move his hand, Wyatt managed to fight the pain and weakly grasp the coffee from Carter. He lifted it to his lips, grimacing whilst he did so.

"Did you hear about what happened in Missouri?" Carter asked. Wyatt darted his eyes around, not knowing whether Carter was talking to him or not. Carter tilted his head over to Wyatt, wanting a response.

"No," Wyatt said, as a drop of blood dripped from his teeth.

"I think maybe two months ago, Jesse James was shot dead there." Carter nodded, "the end of an era, and the end of an incredible story,"

Wyatt was not in the best place, but hearing Carter speak was at least a distraction from the pain and anguish.

"What's your point?" Wyatt muttered. Each time Carter spoke, it could stave off the inevitable beatings.

"Well I used to live in Missouri, when I was no much younger than you, for a couple of years or so. I had to get away from Rockriver for a while." Carter continued. He looked longingly to the distance. "They used to call me the *thunder*." Wyatt rolled his eyes internally, letting Carter gloat about whatever got him into his ivory tower. Carter held Wyatt, waiting for him to ask why.

"Why?" Wyatt caved.

"I used to only do my shooting in a storm," Carter boasted, "so the sounds of rifles blended in. Folks used to shit themselves even in a drizzle." He smiled into the distance some more.

Wyatt took a sip of his cold, rancid coffee, not entertaining Carter's origin story.

"I could compare myself to Jesse James, but one difference stands out," Carter professed. "Maybe even just a year from now, you mark my words," he wiggled his finger in time with his words, "no one will remember the name Jesse James, whereas every time it rains, the whole of Missouri will remember *Henry Carter*."

"Get a hold of yourself," Wyatt managed to spit out, noticing a drop of blood hit the surface of his coffee.

Carter scooted a little closer and grinned through the evening sun's glare, "Do you know what I'm gettin' at?"

"I'm like Jesse James," Wyatt tipped his head down.

"Well not quite," Carter corrected him, "Jesse James died a legend, whereas your story is just sad." Condescendingly, he pouted at Wyatt, adding "and you'll die alone up here, no legacy, no family, just a long history of betrayal, and of course, no wife."

Wyatt's injuries were nothing in comparison to the way he felt about the events that led to this day. Filled with rage, and ready to snap, he calmly placed down his mug on the ground, and fighting all pain, launched his body at Carter. Quickly responding, Al sprung to grab Wyatt's arm, holding him back, whilst Wyatt wriggled violently trying to break free and attack his foe. Exhausted and grunting like a wild beast, what his body had endured began to make a reappearance, and he felt again all the ache in his limbs. Beaten, Wyatt gave up, and without the victory of breaking free from Al, he slumped back down again. Having not moved an inch, Carter laughed as Wyatt settled.

"Wyatt, I like this side of you," he chuckled, "it's *exciting.*" He closed his fist with passion. "We could have really *been* something," Carter shook his head, with mocking disappointment.

It seemed the commotion had woken a little wildlife. Upon the end of the interaction, a quiet rattle came from behind Al. The others looked to see Al stiff and sweating, with his eyes wide hearing the rattle from behind him. Even Wyatt managed to look up. Slowly terrified, Al turned his head behind him to meet the eyes of a coiled snake, its head lifted and curled into the shape of an S, the rattle on its tail raised high and shaking. Its eyes glowed red in the moonlight, and Al beheld the infamous yellow lightning pattern along its back. The Biting Rock Rattlesnake.

"Shit!" Al jumped onto his feet, shaking madly. Al's usually sluggish brain registered that he was face to face with the infamous Biting Rock Rattlesnake, and reflexively he jumped away, cursing loudly. But the snake was faster, springing forward and violently snapping onto Al's ankle. After one tight grip, the snake released him, letting Al drop to the ground gripping his leg and groaning, shaking his head, staring hopelessly into the sky. As the snake slipped away, Carter stood up, drew his revolver, and promptly shot between Al and Billy, killing the snake instantly, it's slithering body immediately halting and breaking almost in two.

Carter leant down to meet Al, and removed his hat solemnly whilst Al rocked back and forth on the ground, his eyes rolling deeper into his skull with every groan.

"A quick, painful death," Carter shook his head. Billy watched over, frightened, but hopeless. Wyatt continued to look down, knowing exactly how Carter would handle the situation. Just as Al's shaking began to fizzle out, Carter stood upright and lifted his gun once more, and pointed it straight between Al's eyes.

"Wait!" Billy came forward with his arms held out, and making his body smaller, he crouched between Carter and Al. "We need to help him!" he pleaded.

"And do what, Billy, you idiot?" Carter's outstretched arm dropped lifelessly, and he stood more casually, irritated by this man in his way.

"I- I don't know, maybe we g- get the venom out, or we could take him back?" Billy asked with hesitation, the question seeming more like he wanted Carter to tell him what to do. "I heard it can take hours, we got time!"

"Go on then, genius." Carter settled his gun by his side, placed a thumb on his belt, and stared intently at Billy, waiting for him to attempt to save Al's life, knowing he and Wyatt may be the only ones who knew it was already too late.

Billy nodded quickly, dropped to his knees and turned to face his dying friend. He wiped his mouth and leant down to Al's ankle. Gripping his lips around the snake bite, he sucked and spat in short, frantic intervals, muttering encouragements to Al as he did so.

Carter sighed and looked at Wyatt sitting with his face to the ground. Impatient, ignoring Billy's frenzied efforts, he stretched his arm out again to aim between Al's frightened, pained eyes, peeking from behind the fumbling, time-wasting Billy. Carter looked away a little, closed his eyes and winced. Al clenched his eyes closed, and the second gunshot shattered the sky. Al's pained movements stopped dead. Billy was left with the lifeless corpse of his friend below him.

Hopeful that the gunshots had spooked any other snakes, Carter sat back down, leaving Al where he lay. Billy stared, white-faced, at the now lifeless Al laying on the ground, try to swallow the tightness in his throat and unable to look at Carter. Billy wriggled back from Al, and tilted his head down as he sat, knowing his own fate would be similar if he were to show any resentment. He curled up, and hugged his knees, hoping Carter wouldn't notice him holding back his tears. Reluctantly accepting Al's fate, though it hurt, he laid himself back to sleep as the evening turned to night. This was the life he'd chosen; by morning, his closest friend would be forgotten.

"Mercy," Carter said.

Wyatt and Carter were left the last men awake, and surrounded by silence, it was almost peaceful despite the presence of a corpse. It made for as good a place as any for a tired Carter to speak further and less violently with Wyatt.

"Are you ready to tell me where Molly is?" Carter broke the calm, quietly, and looked to Wyatt without aggression.

"I don't know," Wyatt lied, avoiding eye contact. Carter sighed, and found it hard to believe Wyatt.

"She dead?" Carter asked, persisting. Wyatt said nothing, he just stared down, finding it difficult to be reminded of Molly again, but unwilling to take responsibility. "I know she is," Carter said, looking away solemnly. This caught Wyatt's attention, perking him up a little, thinking on what kind of audacity Carter must have had to beat him senseless over something he already knew.

"Are you shittin' me?" Wyatt sneered, trying relentlessly to keep himself composed, "you know she's dead?" he said louder gritting his remaining teeth, struggling further to compose himself.

"Yeah I know," Carter squinted his eyes at Wyatt, waiting to watch him snap again.

"Then what the damn *hell* is all this for?!" Wyatt screamed, slamming his coffee cup to the ground, forcing Billy to flinch in his sleep.

"You're a religious man aren't you, Wyatt?" Carter asked, "I just wanted you to be honest, admit it, like God would expect," Carter said, regaining Wyatt's speechlessness.

"But I- I didn't do it," Wyatt recalled, reluctantly, squinting his eyes at the dirt, grounding himself.

"I found Molly's body poorly buried outside that God-forsaken place you were holed up in when we got to you." Carter's voice was now shaky. "Or- or what was left of it," Carter said, choked up, like his own voice didn't want him to say it.

Put off by Carter's sudden interest to confide in him, Wyatt couldn't think of much to say. Carter's comment was simply left to hang in the night's hush, complimented by the mutual memory of Molly's dead body.

Carter lit a cigarette, and passed another to Wyatt, along with the same lit match. Wyatt accepted the temporary truce, and waited blissfully surrounded by smoke for Carter to open his mouth again.

"You just *fucked* everythin' up, huh," Carter said forcefully, shaking his head as he blew out smoke from his nose, whilst a single tear made its way out of his eye. Wyatt was shocked, having not expected this type of conversation to continue, thinking maybe he'd already suffered enough. But Carter was clearly frustrated.

"How do you figure?" Wyatt asked carefully.

"What did I do?!" Carter exploded, "I never lied to you!" Carter's fists were clenched and a vein was bursting from his red forehead. "God *damn*, Wyatt," Carter composed himself, wiped his tear, unclenched his fists, and turned to face Wyatt, who was visibly scared, Carter could almost see Wyatt's heart beating.

"I'm sorry," Wyatt unintentionally whispered. He did try to speak naturally, but he struggled upon seeing Carter so angry.

"Sorry can't help you now, Wyatt," Carter wiped his hands over his face, readjusting his emotions to maintain his control, "you know I'm a man of my word and in the Lord's name you will suffer for your sins."

Carter preached as if he were the righteous hand of God. Still fearful, Wyatt allowed Carter to continue in his delusion, after all, there wasn't much point in fighting. Carter was right, Wyatt had ruined everything for himself from a certain perspective. He'd witnessed endless misfortune all for the sake of a certain death at the top of Biting Rock. The only solace that could've come from this was his wife's safety, but being held hostage in the wild was not the best place to witness it, and therefore it wasn't guaranteed to him.

"Where's your brother, Wyatt?" Carter asked, calmer once again, "did you ever find him?" Wyatt didn't want to hear this question, and his anxiety augmented. Carter sat still, watching Wyatt for any giveaways, or movements he could question.

"I can only assume you found him, or you'd never have run," Carter pressed. "But when we got to you, Joe wasn't there. Where was he? Maybe he was the burned up second body outside the building, or is that another of your innocent victims?"

"He never came back," Wyatt tried his best not to stutter, "I was alone, I killed Molly, and an innocent witness." He was shaking, and peeked upwards to check whether Carter's expression showed belief or dubiety.

"Are you lying to me?" Carter asked smirking, entertained by Wyatt's faith in his lies, "why do you have to lie for him? What's he ever done for you?" His questions were beginning to irk Wyatt.

"He's family," Wyatt murmured.

"Oh family," Carter chortled to himself, "didn't stop you tearin' mine apart."

"I said I'm sorry," Wyatt insisted, but knew the effort was futile.

"You know, Wyatt," Carter continued, "you're always tryin' to act like everything you do is for someone else," he spat. "Joe, or *Holy* Mary, surely among others, but really, everything you do is all about *you*." He pointed sharply at Wyatt's chest.

"That's not true," Wyatt fought his own side.

"It is true, you just miss the *old days*," Carter interrupted, "and it's got you nowhere," he chuckled and waved his arms around gesturing the narrow canyon around them, "*literally* nowhere!"

"Damn you," Wyatt said under his breath, sick of being criticised.

"Damn me?! Ha!" Carter laughed, "You done damned yourself, son! Look around!" He leant closer to Wyatt, smiling, pointing, and enjoying the opportunity to speak freely. "Is this your ranch? Is this Mary's dream? Is this Joe's dream?" he mocked. Wyatt felt a jolt in his soul each time Carter listed another failure.

"This has nothing to do with Joe *or* Mary," Wyatt pleaded.

"Oh, but it does," Carter proclaimed, "this is your lesson, Wyatt, Mary knows better now than to settle for the likes of a *sinner*." His words pierced Wyatt's heart, until Wyatt wished he were being physically beaten again instead.

"Please," Wyatt didn't want to take anymore, sinking back inside, fighting the confrontation.

"And Joe?" Carter ignored Wyatt's pleas for mercy, "well that's a classic." He leant back. "Straight from the good book, almost perfect, seeing as you have just then been given the opportunity for confession," he preached, waiting for Wyatt to take the bait. Wyatt looked up with the eyes of a pup, but the conscience of a sinner.

Carter stood and towered over Wyatt, and with the moonlight rested behind his head, he donned his hat once more to hide his face in shadow.

"And God said unto Cain!" Carter bellowed, and placed his hand on his holster, "where is thy brother Abel?" His eyes became visible, reflecting the stars in the night sky as Wyatt looked up at them, "are you your brother's keeper, Wyatt?"

7: Silverfish Ranch

Silverfish Ranch, Texas, 1876

Just one day away from the age of 18, and Joe was already a behemoth of a man. Under his layer of fat, was pure overgrown muscle. His size was juxtaposed by his suave nature, and contradicted yet again by his youthful exuberance. A young man on the verge of peaking as an adult, his future was promising. Every day Wyatt looked at his younger brother, and thought about how proud he was of his brother's potential as a rancher, and how much he enjoyed mentoring him and sculpting him into a better version of himself.

At 7am every morning, Wyatt and Joe headed to the fields to find the cows fresh patches of grass, and to keep the bulls at bay. The sunrise laid a shimmer on the grass every morning without fail. It was the little things, life was good, and it was pure happiness at Silverfish Ranch.

"Are you gettin' me a birthday gift?" Joe nudged Wyatt, tightening his overalls as they both walked the path toward the cows. Wyatt squinted, because the sun was behind Joe's head, and despite its size, it didn't quite block the light.

"I got a couple things, you're lucky I partake in such a tradition," Wyatt chuckled, "like women." He knew Joe would be grateful with anything, but Wyatt always wanted more for him. Their feet crunched on leaves as they walked.

"And are you gettin' me a nice girl?" Joe laughed, with an ounce of sincerity, whilst donning thick gloves preparing for work.

"I think you had enough already," Wyatt smiled, "maybe move out your mama's house first."

The tracks at the ranch were long, but neither of them minded the walking most days. Some days they simply just forgot the horses, and enjoyed each other's company for longer. Walking, sitting, smoking, and then they'd tell the boss there was a coyote related emergency, or some other terrible excuse for doing less work.

As they approached the grass covered fence surrounding the cows, Joe slapped Wyatt's back and smiled as he jogged forward and vaulted over.

"Cows ain't gonna feed themselves, big bro," he said jauntily as he made it to the other side, eager to begin the working day. Wyatt laughed and opened the gate just feet away from where Joe had hurdled, and walked through, following his brother into the bright green field.

Each day was fairly similar. Typically, the ranch owner left Joe and Wyatt to their own devices on most days, trusting that they'd work well together, and he'd be right every time. Unlike the other ranch hands, Joe and Wyatt were productive, and enjoyed working, talking for hours, and taking great pride in their bond and their jobs. Even after a day's work, they were inseparable, and would continue together to do whatever would take place in the evenings, usually involving a great deal of whiskey-fuelled exploring, or unruly behaviour to make extra money.

Hours passed in the same field, and the midday sun was heating the brothers' hats as they sat in deck chairs hidden safely by the field's distance from the other workers, taking a break with a pair of secretive beers.

"I think once mama's better, we should open our own ranch," Joe said, taking a swig and slouching down.

So optimistic, Wyatt thought. The optimism was refreshing, so he didn't deprive Joe of that. He definitely didn't have the stomach to tell him that tuberculosis did not have too positive of a recovery rate. Wyatt just sat and mirrored Joe, allowing his serenity to radiate positivity.

"The Wilson brothers ranch," Wyatt engaged with Joe's idea.

"The Joseph Wilson ranch," Joe replied with a cheeky smirk, "you can be a ranch hand, of course," he teased.

"Hell no, you need me for the brains," Wyatt laughed, gently mocking his younger brother, placing the empty bottle on the ground before standing up, groaning and stretching.

"Oh, come on, one more!" Joe insisted, stretching out his words.

"Got to wait 'til next year now," Wyatt grinned, as he picked up the shovel from the floor. "Gotta scoop shit. Happy birthday," he laughed, as he walked to where the cows had huddled. Joe sighed and sunk a little further into his chair, watching his brother leave, before huffing and regaining his enthusiasm, following Wyatt.

As they shovelled inside the cow pen, they were both well acquainted enough to enjoy a shared silence, just comfortable in each other's company. The work was not only for them, but for their mother, who was unable to take on paid work, with her in such a poor state. Each penny went towards paying to keep the three of them content. On most days however, it wasn't quite enough.

"You want me to spoil a gift early?" Wyatt smiled at Joe over the pasture.

"Oh, sure," Joe said, with a smile, ready for a bit of fun.

Wyatt presented a small sheet of paper from his pocket and held it up in Joe's eye-line. It had a mean face printed poorly but accurately in the centre, with the words *Ellis Wood* at the top, and *Wanted Dead or Alive* at the bottom, *$300 reward.* The face was angry, and feral in appearance. This was a man who had not groomed, and looked as though he ate his meals whilst they were still alive.

"Mean sum' bitch, huh?" Joe laughed as he looked back down and continued to shovel, "I'm in."

"They call him the *savage*," Wyatt chuckled, "I got word from the saloon that he's campin' in the canyon by Gold River. We can go tonight," Wyatt said putting the poster back into his jeans.

"Indian territory?" Joe stopped shovelling and stood tall, "I ain't got a death wish, Wyatt," he said as his eyes widened, adjusting his hat.

"Oh, there ain't hardly any Indians left, Joe, and who's to say they're still in the canyon?" Wyatt shrugged off Joe's concern, "quick job, in and out, hog killin' time, Ellis thrown on the back of a horse, payday," he said with rhythm.

"How can you know?" Joe dropped the shovel and approached Wyatt with his arms crossed, questioning the idea.

"Well, I guess that's the fun part, ain't it," Wyatt grinned, "what's life without a little gamblin'?"

The hours dragged on, this time with the excitement of a hunt the next day. On their walk away from the fields, the sun began to set, and they pondered a plan for tomorrow.

"Game plan?" Joe asked. Wyatt was confident that the two of them could handle this themselves.

"I've borrowed two repeaters, and plenty of rounds from Mr Sawyer. Don't tell mama," Wyatt explained. "The two of us can ride into the canyon in silence, and take whoever's there out before they realise what hit 'em. We'll camp out closer to them tonight."

"Well, I guess that's better than guns blazin'," Joe laughed sarcastically.

"We can peek down through the trees first to make sure of the numbers," Wyatt replied.

"Dead or alive?" Joe asked, "I'm itchin' for a bit of fun, come on."

"Dead," Wyatt said quickly, "I'm too tired to babysit, and long as these hands work, I'm pullin' the trigger."

The sky turned and swirled as the sun began to set, presenting the sunny yet shadowy canvas in which the infamous Wilson brothers usually get to work. During their walk away from the fields, Joe's mind began to think creatively again.

"Just Wilson Ranch," he smiled into the distance. Wyatt shared a smile, and directed his eyes into the same nirvana where Joe stared.

"Wilson Ranch," Wyatt smiled, "me, you and mama."

"Can't wait," their smiles persisted, and it was this kind of happiness that made a dream possible. It didn't matter about the means, only the end.

~

Later that evening, the Wilson brothers settled for the night in an open stretch of land. It was dark with no shelter, but the weather was pleasant. No wind, and no clouds, and the sky a canvass of stars.

"Do you ever think of anything up there?" Joe said quietly, staring up, as Wyatt struck a match on a pile of sticks and twigs on the ground. There were a couple of blankets laid on the dirt, one under Joe, and one for Wyatt to sit back on once the fire was lit.

"No," Wyatt said, still trying to get a twig to adopt the match's flame.

"I do," Joe continued to stare at the sky, moving his neck around trying to catch a glimpse of each corner of it. "I hear stories," he muttered.

"Oh yeah?" Wyatt strained, leaning further over the pile of sticks, poking his hand into it to light a twig at the base. "Tell me one, and I'll tell you if it's bullshit."

"Some folk say they sometimes see people in the sky," Joe murmured, focused on the stars, "and they make bad things happen to bad people."

"People in the sky?" Wyatt sniggered, as a twig caught alight. He pulled his hand out, letting the fire catch on, and he shuffled backwards to sit on the blanket that awaited him.

"Yeah, I believe it," Joe looked back down to Wyatt.

"Why?" Wyatt asked, laying down onto his back uninterested, and placing his hat over his face.

"Some people seen them," Joe looked back upwards with bewilderment, "when the sun is up."

"Some people's lives are boring, Joe. They make stuff up. A whole bunch of horseshit, and the worst smellin' shit gets the most attention," Wyatt replied, muffled under his hat. "Well, the least attention from me, that's for sure."

"Folk call them the *dark watchers*," Joe said, "and they appear before you die, or before someone else dies."

"But you said it was when the sun is up," Wyatt muttered. "Why call them *dark* watchers?"

"Oh," Joe responded, a little stumped.

"See?" Wyatt chuckled, "it's all just stories," he sighed as he settled a little more.

"I prefer to believe in it," Joe looked to Wyatt's covered face. "Sometimes I think I see them, before I kill someone. I ain't sure if they're judgin' me, or warnin' me, I ain't sure. Hell, I ain't even sure I seen 'em, I just know it sure does get hot and confusin' sometimes."

"Uh-huh," Wyatt murmured quietly, trying to fall asleep.

"Ain't no one seen 'em up close," Joe continued, "they disappear."

"How convenient," Wyatt sighed sarcastically, "magic dark watchers that you can't see. Get some sleep." He rolled over onto his side away from Joe.

Joe looked up again, smiling. He chuckled to himself and laid back, still staring.

"Do you ever think what we do is wrong?" Joe continued, as Wyatt let out a mildly irritated sigh.

"Yeah," Wyatt mumbled, taking the hat from off his face, reluctantly accepting Joe's conversational mood.

"It's fun though, huh?" Joe gave him a weak smile.

"We shouldn't, but right now we have to." Wyatt stared up at the night sky, "once we get enough, we'll get out of here and won't have to do it no more."

"I ain't scared of no dark watchers, Wyatt," Joe said.

"That ain't the point I'm makin', Joe," Wyatt sighed again. The fire flickered out, after only burning for a few seconds.

"You can't burn shit," Joe chuckled, coaxing a lighter mood from Wyatt, expecting Wyatt to try again. But he didn't, he just continued to lay back.

"At least no one saw," he tittered under his hat.

8: The Vulture

Outside a Native American settlement, Texas, evening, the next day, 1876

Over the years, a horse learns to obey commands without the command even being vocalised. It can align its own choices with its owner's, having been trained so well. Wyatt's horse, Banjo, was like an extension of himself. The slightest movement of his foot could make Wyatt's intentions clear to Banjo.

Despite Joe being a little younger, his horse was much bigger in order to support his weight. Because of his size, Joe had continually needed to ride bigger horses to keep up with his growing, and thus he was not as bonded to his horse. Boss, the horse that Joe sat upon, was skittish in comparison to Banjo, and Joe had trouble keeping him still, whilst they stared down at the Indian settlement from atop the canyon.

"Can you see from here?" asked Joe as Boss tapped his feet. The brothers were some distance away, and could just make out the shapes of many teepees and a small fire inside the canyon, and hoped they wouldn't be spotted.

"A bit," said Wyatt, looking down at the thick, tall trees amongst and surrounding the tents, shielding most of his vision on the settlement.

"Trees ain't helping," muttered Joe, baffled by the idea of a small forest growing inside a dry canyon. "Still a lot more Indians than I hoped for though." In the distant camp, a handful of people could be seen by a fire, and Joe was concerned about the sections of the camp that he couldn't see.

"Should we risk it?" Wyatt looked over at Joe, "hell, it's only bows and arrows, right?" He smiled nervously, trying to calm himself.

"Just as dangerous in the right hands, Wyatt." Joe was concerned, not entirely convinced it was a good idea. They both stared a little more intently at the settlement, looking for their target.

"That him?" Wyatt pointed, shielding his eyes from the late evening sun with his other hand. Joe copied and tipped his hat down to block the sun.

"Yeah, must be," Joe drawled, "long hair, dirty, only sum' bitch with a hat."

"Times like this, I wish I could shoot from this distance," Wyatt laughed. His laid-back approach to the hit was somewhat calming for his brother. Boss was becoming impatient underneath Joe, and his huffing became more frequent.

"Calm down, boy," Joe said to his horse, not quite perfecting the horse's preferred intonation.

"Is that gonna be a problem?" Wyatt asked, encouraging Joe to keep ahold of Boss.

"No, no, I got him," Joe mumbled as he concentrated on reigning in the horse, eventually, and slowly, calming Boss back down, "he's just impatient."

Above the canyon, a lone vulture screeched as it circled the camp below. Each flap of its giant wings thumped and kept its heavy body in the sky between each glide.

"Talk about bad omens," Joe muttered, watching the vulture.

"These Indians is savages, and the bird knows it, Joe," Wyatt studied the vulture, "he's just waitin' for a meal."

"You sure 'bout this, Wyatt?" Joe asked, superstitiously.

"I'm sure," Wyatt sighed, "let's move before it gets too dark."

Wyatt gently jolted the reigns, and Banjo began to slowly and quietly walk to the trees shrouding the downhill path into the canyon. The trees were tall and stood straight, but thick with leaves and branches – with many obstacles, and good places to hide. Joe gave one last look at the ways behind him, but sighed and turned to follow Wyatt.

"Well, I sure can't leave you alone," Joe muttered under his breath, only a handful of steps behind his brother.

As they delved deeper in the canyon, the trees became denser. The only thing that implied they were still going in the right direction was the dry path ahead of them, gently sloping downhill. That and the vulture, moving ever closer above them.

"Shush!" Wyatt came to sudden halt, raising his hand to Joe behind him.

"What-,"

"Shush!" Wyatt interrupted more forcefully, "you hear that?" He looked quiet and confused. The vulture that had been circling above, was now nowhere to be seen.

A timid snap came from within the trees to their left, the only sound for minutes.

"There it is again," Wyatt insisted. He looked into the trees but couldn't see a thing.

"Wyatt..." Joe said almost silently, staring widely at the path ahead past Wyatt. Wyatt turned away from the trees to face forward again, to be met by the menacing eyes of the vulture, sitting patiently at the end of the trail, just before the path took a corner. Its shadow was huge covering the whole width of the path, the evening sunset casting it almost directly from the side.

"What's he doin'?" Wyatt whispered slowly to himself, staring back into the vulture's eyes. Its head tilted, and another snap came from the trees beside the path. Wyatt and Joe's heads bounced quickly back to the trees, and like deer in the crossfire, they were left speechless and still.

A man emerged slowly from the trees alone, his face covered with dirt, and framed by a headdress made from feathers, not unlike a vulture's. Switching and flitting his glance between Wyatt and Joe, the man held eye contact with both brothers simultaneously. Edging closer to the path in front of them, one hand held a bow, whilst the other pulled the string back halfway. A fierce, barbed arrow pointed to the ground. He seemed to not only be native to America, but native to this forest in the canyon.

He stood between the brothers and the vulture, maintaining his glare. He pulled an inch further on the bows string, and Wyatt's stiffness invisibly turned to readiness.

"*Bird. Protect. Nest*," the man spoke. His voice was deep, and gravelly, like he was dehydrated.

"*Did you get that?*" Joe whispered to Wyatt, confused, as Boss huffed and began to shuffle his feet.

"You understand me?" Wyatt spoke up. The man fell silent briefly, breathing calmly.

"*Chief. Teach,*" he continued, his accent thick with difficulty. He held his gaze on Wyatt and the grip wrapped on his bow tightened. "*Tribe. Bird,*" the man nodded to the trees.

"We don't want the bird," Wyatt said, beginning to sweat. Something about the man ahead of them was frightening; the way he appeared so calm, yet so ready to defend a lowly bird.

"*Drop. Gun,*" the man growled. Wyatt peeked over at Joe, who looked unsettled. He gave Joe a small nod, and the brothers obliged. Slowly and carefully, they removed the repeaters that were hung on their backs, then threw them quickly to the ground. Hopefully, this man remained unaware of the revolvers attached to their belts, out of the man's sight. The sound of metal hitting the forest floor sparked discontent in Joe's horse, and he began to stomp.

"Boss, settle down, boy," Joe insisted as he struggled with the reigns. Boss huffed and ignored Joe continuing to stomp.

"*Joe, stop,*" Wyatt hissed, as the native man ahead of them pulled the string farther from his bow.

"I'm tryin', Wyatt, damn!" Joe protested. The rise in volume startled the native, who pulled his bow true, and quickly pointed it directly at Joe, debating whether to stand his ground or turn and run from the unpredictable horse. Startled by the certain danger, Boss reared, nearly throwing Joe from his back, letting out a panicked whinny, and waving his front hooves in the air.

As Boss landed back on his feet, the lone tribesman took a small and careful step back, and the vulture flew away, releasing a mighty screech. Boss, with Joe on his back, bolted directly at the man ahead of him.

"Joe, no!" Wyatt yelled, but it was no use. Joe could not tame his horse now, and it trampled directly over the panicked native man. The underside of Boss was splattered by the blood of the man, as a hoof slammed through his skull. Boss continued to charge down the path and galloped around the corner. "Hyaa!" Wyatt bellowed as he whipped Banjo's reigns and chased after Joe.

The path twisted, Wyatt and Banjo put everything into every step to catch up to Joe while the trees sped past them on either side, dodging and ducking the overhanging and stray branches. Just out of reach, Boss and Joe could be seen hurtling further into the small encampment that hosted the native tribe. Before Boss could go further, he tripped and whinnied, tumbling into the ground and throwing Joe head over heels ahead of him. Joe landed suddenly on his own head, hitting the ground with a harsh smack, his body flopping to motionless.

Halting Banjo, Wyatt leapt from his back and ran to Joe. He knelt down beside him, and grabbed his arms.

"Joe?! Joe?!" he pleaded, trying to shake his brother awake.

"Wyatt," Joe croaked weakly. Wyatt sighed in relief, his brother was alive, but barely conscious. He looked up to see Boss, face down in the dirt, with two arrows impaled directly in his shoulder.

"Shit..." Wyatt muttered as he let go of Joe, clocking the arrows. Skeptically, he looked around. He slowly rose to his feet, and prepared his hand to pull the gun from his side. Rustling came from the trees again, this time louder than before. Slowly, but surely, the tribe began to appear, emerging one by one from the evening shadows, heavily armed. They had them surrounded.

"Okay, you gotta wake up now," said Wyatt quickly, turning his attention back to Joe, and kneeling down again he shook him faster. Joe flopped limply in Wyatt's arms. "Dammit," Wyatt cursed and gave up - there was no time for Joe. He looked around again at the natives closing in on him.

Okay, Wyatt, he thought to himself, trying to calm down and compose himself, *time to show these folk what you're made of.* He only had 6 bullets in his gun, and there would be no time to reload. Adrenaline rushed through his veins, and like lightning, he dived to the dead horse, simultaneously pulling his gun from its holster. The horse became a temporary shield from those now behind him, as he locked eyes with those directly in front of him. With one hand on the trigger, and the other on the hammer, he fired 3 speedy shots, killing the three closest men instantly and leaving perfect bleeding holes in their foreheads. Arrows began to fly over Wyatt's head, and he desperately pressed further into Boss's cadaver.

To his right, he could see the few had become many, and the horse could not protect him forever. He turned to face ahead and stretched his arm to aim. *Three bullets left,* he thought, relentlessly racking his brain for subsequent ideas.

Bang! Another dead, *two bullets left,* **Bang!** Outnumbered, his palm sweat loosened the grip on his gun. *One more, take care of Mama, Joe.* Hopeless and trapped, he took another look at Joe and aimed to fire at the approaching crowd ahead of him.

"Ah!" Wyatt cried out and winced, dropping his gun before his last shot could be fired. A sharp pain had fired through his hand. Through the adrenaline filled haze, he looked at his hand to see it pinned against Boss's carcass, with blood dripping from the arrow splintered through it. He turned his head to the left, and through his scared eyes, he saw a lone tribesman, with an empty bow pointed straight at him.

The tribe circled in on Wyatt, a couple poking at Joe's limp body. Wyatt dropped his head, hand still attached to the horse by an arrow. He knew that he'd been beat. The shooter looked down on him, and blocked the evening sunset. Wyatt lifted his gaze to his assailant, and wondered if these were his last minutes.

"Son of a-," Before Wyatt finished, a blow came to his head, and everything went black. Drifting out of touch, Wyatt's last vision was an angry victim with a big rock…

9: Ellis 'The Savage' Wood

The Native American settlement, Texas, 1876

Wyatt's eyes began to open up, but they weren't as effective as he'd hoped. It was dark, with only a campfire and the moon as light. Surrounded by trees, he was disoriented, but gradually he struggled awake, and found himself bound to a tree trunk, unable to move. He was sat, that much was clear, the vast ropes keeping his arms at his side and his chest held tight against the rough bark. The pain in his hand was unbearable. His first lucid thought was of Joe, but it was too dark to see if he were there with him.

"Joe?" Wyatt whispered, trying not to alert the few people that sat by a campfire in view. It was very quiet, but murmurs of conversation came from the fire.

"Wyatt?" Joe replied from the darkness on Wyatt's right just feet away, and relief could be heard through his quiet tone. "Where are we, Wyatt?" Joe continued to whisper.

"I ain't sure," Wyatt kept his voice down, "must be the Indian settlement."

"God damn," Joe whispered a little louder. "Told you so," he muttered. Murmurs from the fire picked up, and through the darkness, their eyes became visible to the brothers. In unfamiliar language, the tribe spoke to one another whilst staring at the tree-bound brothers, before turning and retiring to a single tent, which glowed reflecting the fire.

"It'll be alright, Joe, hang in there," Wyatt said, waiting for the tent to open up again. He could feel Joe moving the hard ground with his wriggling, "just stay calm."

"I don't like this one bit, Wyatt, we gotta go, my head hurts," Joe whimpered, trying harder and harder to break free. Wyatt stayed still, knowing he'd have no chance of squirming free from these ropes. He did consider however, chewing through it.

Joe continued to violently strain within the ropes, whilst the tent opened back up. The tribe emerged, and with them, another man with a lantern. This man and a handful of tribesmen approached the trees where Wyatt and Joe were bound. As they got closer, the lantern illuminated the face of the man, revealing a sinister, dirty smile, and yellow, tired eyes. His face twitched, as flies jumped on and off his skin.

"Fresh *meat*," he announced, stopping a few feet in front of them, and lighting up the area with his lantern. His voice was guttural and grating, each word heavy and protracted, his rotten teeth adding an excess of spit as the words left his mouth. The lantern emitted a comforting, welcome light, at odds with the meance of the man wielding it, and the brothers could see each other again. Joe was sweating, with drops falling from his face every time he took a deep, fast breath. It was clear now that this familiar man was not like the other tribesmen. He stank of dirt, sweat, and death. "I have caught the legendary Wilson Brothers!" the man laughed with grating energy, a chorus of chuckles from his tribe gathered near him. He leant in closer and crouched, creating a triad of the brothers and himself. "I am *Chief,*" he drooled through his rancid teeth.

"You're Ellis Wood," Wyatt muttered. Ellis darted his head to Wyatt and his smile immediately dissipated, his brow furrowed, and the lantern shone on his yellow eyes, going from amusement to utter ferocity in a heartbeat.

"Quiet, bitch!" Ellis yelled, swinging his free hand at Wyatt, and landing a crisp backhanded slap on his cheek. Ellis stared at Wyatt briefly after the slap, but promptly widened his eyes again and renewed his smile, turning to Joe. "Big feller, you may speak," he grinned, more drool spilling from his lips. Confused, Joe looked back, bewildered by such rapid conflicting emotions within one man.

"You're Ellis Wood," Joe copied Wyatt. He was met with a brief, tense silence, followed by Ellis Wood leaning to enter Joe's personal space.

"*I am,*" Ellis growled slowly, edging closer to Joe, his stench stronger and stinging Joe's nostrils, "did you come here to kill me?" Ellis asked with a patronising frown.

"We ain't finished yet," Joe hissed back, as he gave his ropes another nudge.

"*Us neither,*" Ellis sneered and inched even closer to Joe's face, his spit dripping onto Joe's stretched out legs below. Joe backed his face away a little, with his hair pressed into the tree. But Ellis only got closer, emitting a quiet growl as he continued glaring. "I'm gonna have *fun* with *y'all*," his eyes slowly gyrated back over at Wyatt, still inches from Joes face. His stare was that of a mad man's, piercing the soul of those who bear witness. Wyatt hid his fear, and ignored the speed of his heart, reluctantly holding eye contact with Ellis, who just continued to smile and slobber.

"Lay one finger on him and I'll snap you in half," Wyatt said calmly, masking the anxiety.

"Boy," Ellis taunted, "you're goin' nowhere, *hole hand,*" he retracted from Joe's breathing space, and plopped down to face them both. No response was given to his juvenile insult. "Right about now, my boys should be about a minute's ride away from your home, and your mama," he smirked, his smirk turning into a giggle.

"Wh-..." Wyatt tried to squeeze out a word. The fear of what Ellis may say next left him almost speechless.

"They gon' kill her!" Ellis laughed. His laugh echoed among the tribe. "You mess with The Savage, you pay the price!" He laughed again before at growling the ends of his sentences, as if two emotions were fighting for the limelight, or two people inside just one very unhinged man.

"What...?" Wyatt muttered.

"*What?*" Ellis mocked, and continued with his breathy chuckle, "What can I say? I'm a rascal! Think I don't know you boys too?!" he bellowed, forcing a laugh through the mucus that filled his lungs.

"W- why? How?" Wyatt stuttered, and his panic began to show.

"*W- w- w-,*" Ellis copied, laughed, and slapped his knee. He switched again, and anger came through, "you can't even *speak* no good!" His laughter was absent now, and the menacing stare and growl returned, "some *legendary* brothers," he mocked.

"My mama?" Joe mumbled incoherently under his breath, his head had dropped to face his lap.

"Speak up, big Joe!" Ellis spat as he turned his attention back over to Joe.

"My mama?!" Joe looked up and shouted. His teeth were gritted, and he matched Ellis's violent stare.

"Joe?" Wyatt asked, worried. Joe took no notice and continued to hyperventilate through his teeth, holding a murderous stare on the feral man in front of him.

"My *mama*?!" he shouted louder, shaking, and nudging the ropes around him.

Ellis stood and laughed throughout, dancing a small jig for the joy that another man's anger brings.

"You can't save her!" Ellis danced and mocked in time with his steps, laughing at the brothers' misfortune.

"You *evil* son of a bitch!" Joe yelled, shaking even more violently and persistently at his ropes.

"Joe, stop," Wyatt hissed, frightened. "We're outnumbered," he said quieter.

Joe ignored Wyatt again, the heartbeat in his chest was fast and loud, and with each thud, another fearful thought of his mother came to mind. And with each thought, another possessed dream of murdering this monster of a man became more prominent.

"You can't save her! You can't save her!" Ellis's sing-song taunting rattled the mind of young Joe. Joe strained harder, and harder with each motif of Ellis's twisted chant.

With one last tug, Joe stopped, slumped, and with effort, composed his breathing.

The taunting stopped.

"Joe?" Wyatt said in the silence, as Ellis stared confused at a potential beast in repose.

Calmly breathing, Joe lifted his head to look at Ellis again.

"Cat got your tongue?" Ellis asked quietly, "give up?" Although seeming calmer, Joe's eyes twitched, not able to wipe any tears, and he forced breath through his nostrils, getting faster.

Wyatt gazed at his brother, heart pounding. Wyatt thought Joe was a fairly gentle man, although he never wanted Joe to lose his temper, because if he did, he *did. Don't lose your cool, Joe,* he thought, internally praying. It was unprecedented to Wyatt that Joe would ever use his full strength and potential to hurt another human being. Although possible, Wyatt didn't want to see it.

With a sudden rapid breath, and like a bear, Joe sprung to his feet, roaring in anger, finally breaking the ropes and sending them soaring to either side as he yelled in frustration. Every man stepped back, but Ellis only grinned, as the mountain of a man barrelled towards him, eyes like fire and arms like logs.

"Shit!" Wyatt exclaimed, again wriggling at his ropes frantically, praying the sweat would at least help, in a desperate attempt to stop his rage-fuelled adolescent brother.

"Ha ha! Come on, boy!" Ellis shrieked with glee, watching this nightmare man just steps away, his arms cocked above his head ready to smash skulls. Ellis maintained eye contact and smiled, whilst he stretched his arm out to the side, gesturing any tribesman to hand him a weapon. Nobody did, they kept their distance.

Arrows flew at Joe, just scraping his skin, some barely piercing the fat around his body, as no man dared to get closer. In the panicked frenzy, the native tribe could not aim accurately. Approaching his captor, Joe slammed his fists into Ellis' shoulders. They landed like two boulders, likely snapping Ellis' collar bones, and dropping him to his knees where he then flopped onto his side, groaning, and trying to roll. Joe turned to Wyatt for a moment and was unrecognisable. However, upon seeing his brother, his eyes widened and blood slowed through his veins once more. He turned from Ellis, and ran to Wyatt, promptly grabbing the rope around the tree, pulling hard, and snapping the line that held Wyatt dormant. Wyatt then sprang to action and grabbed his brother's arms.

"Let's go, now!" he yelled keeping Joe facing him, and attempting to pull him away from their captors with his remaining good hand, before anyone reacted to their escape.

Flying through the tribe and trees, thankfully protected by dark and obstacles, Wyatt and Joe made haste for an exit, followed closely by the tribe who had given chase. Wyatt whistled for Banjo as they ran, hoping he'd find them in their time of desperate need. It was still dark, and it was down to the grace of God that they not trip or crash.

In the camp, Ellis was pulled to his feet, and the brothers could hear his cries from the distance.

"I'll find you, Wilsons!" Ellis screamed from the forest, "I'll hunt you all down!" The cries became quieter as Joe and Wyatt neared the surrounding path of the canyon, nearly drowned out by their own heavy footsteps and the wind flying past them.

"...and your wives! And your children! And your children's children!" came Ellis's enraged echoes through the trees.

Banjo sped through the trees to the rescue, ahead of the flighting brothers. *Thank God,* Wyatt thought, laying to rest the sub-conscious feeling that Banjo had ran away or been killed. But no, Banjo was a loyal and strong friend.

"On the horse, Joe!" Wyatt yelled as they sprinted to Banjo, who was kicking his feet ready to bolt, ready to take the brothers' weight and power through. Wyatt vaulted the saddle and landed on the horse's back, searing pain rushing through his crippled hand as he gripped the reigns.

"I swear, that wasn't me, Wyatt," Joe panted as he jumped up on Banjo behind Wyatt, "I don't know what that was. And my head hurts!" he groaned. Banjo felt the weight push him down, huffed, persisted, and stood up straight ready to run.

"I know, buddy, now let's burn the *fuckin'* breeze!" Wyatt exclaimed as he swung his arms to kickstart Banjo's sprint for freedom.

"We get mama?" Joe asked as they rode up the path into the night. Wyatt was shocked by Joe's unusually poor grammar, but ignored it nonetheless for his brother who would likely now be shaken. Banjo's hooves provided a constant therapeutic beat to their words.

"No, Joe, we need to run, listen to Banjo and calm down," Wyatt said with uncertainty, and reconsidered his attitude, "I'm sorry, buddy, I think she's long gone now, we can't risk goin' back home."

"You don't know that!" Joe yelled over Wyatt's head, louder than Banjo's hooves.

"We need to run, Joe!" Wyatt shouted, "we run, or we stay and die!"

"Wyatt no!" Joe reached round to try and grab the reigns. With a struggle, Wyatt elbowed back.

"Joe!" he screamed, "we will die!" Joe caved, and settled his arms. In the silence and galloping, Wyatt held control of Banjo. Joe planted his face in Wyatt's back, quietly sobbing, and gripping Wyatt's waist for comfort. The war-torn brothers rode into the night, seeking sanctuary in whatever far away town would take them, far from the threat of Ellis 'The Savage' Wood and his tribe of Native Americans.

~

Days passed on horseback. They slept in small towns on their way, some were perfect, but nowhere seemed far enough. California was as far to the west as could be, and California is where the brothers would soon find Rockriver; a small town with a quiet brook, sheltered from the sun by a large rock. There read a sign: "Home to the rarest rattlesnake in the states." A thrill seeker's dream.

10: The Sasquatch Hunt

The Woods, North of Meller Creek, California, January, 1880

After passing Meller Creek on horseback, the woods became larger after a long journey, they appeared vast before Wyatt's eyes glowing green in the midday light. The trees were tall, and seemed not to end as Wyatt looked left and right. He held Banjo back, as he'd become unsettled and restless seeing the maze before him. It was undeniably the farthest Wyatt had ventured from home since moving to Rockriver, and the first time he'd been back to any forest since the unfortunate events of 1876.

Having come straight from making his deal with Carter, Wyatt's confidence was still ahead of his morals, and he felt it too late to turn back now. He'd made it this far, and had to persist, if only to make betraying Mary somehow worthwhile.

Looking to his left, he saw Carter's father's brewery in the distance.

I'll start there.

Upon learning of the brewery's employees hunting a 'monster', he knew that starting close to them would be his best bet in navigating the woods to find Joe.

A group of old fallen trees, he quoted Carter in his head. *That could be anywhere, dammit.*

With a whip of the reins, he and Banjo made haste alongside the border of the woods. Wyatt racked his brain relentlessly as to what he could say to Joe. It had been so long, and Joe was not the same man anymore. Since the death of their mother and his fall from horseback, Joe had lost all sense of his personality. Having refused to mourn, he had reverted back to a state of childlike innocence, and toddler-like impatience coupled with emotional fragility. In short, Joe spent his short time in Rockriver depressed, unhinged, and angry. Wyatt was wise enough not to expect the same Joe from Silverfish Ranch, and instead to prepare for the man that Rockriver feared, the man who destroyed Ida's saloon in a fit of rage before quickly running for the woods. Wanted dead or alive by every local, who collectively were none the wiser of the man Joe used to be. Wyatt and Joe presumed their mother dead on the day they fled to Rockriver, meaning to the townsfolk, Joe had always been this way.

With it being midday, the brewery was open and functioning. Wyatt thought it wise to keep his forest snooping on the down low, so as to not alert any hunters. He tied Banjo to a tree about a quarter mile from the brewery, which still looked large despite its distance.

"Good boy," he said, patting Banjo's neck before leaving. Banjo nuzzled in and sighed before allowing Wyatt's departure. "Won't be long," said Wyatt, hoping that was true.

Wyatt looked through the trees to behold the all too familiar labyrinth that a forest can be. He bent down to remove the spurs from his boots, for the jingle would not be welcome here. Pulling a branch to the side, he began his walk through the dense woodland, stepping over roots and crunching the dead leaves with his footsteps.

Further into the woods the mixed sounds of birds echoed with the quiet clanking and humming of the machines in the brewery. Wyatt looked for every fallen tree, but they were more common than he'd expected, and not one hid his brother. By the time an hour had passed, Wyatt was deep into the forest, with only the placement of the sun to guide his way back. Come nightfall, navigating back to Banjo would be a problem.

Finally, near a drift of dead trees, Wyatt spotted a natural cave formation in a small crater, with its entrance sheltered with twigs and branches, unnaturally fashioned into a canopy. Judging by the fresh smoke coming from a burnt pile of sticks outside the cave, it seemed that a fire had been lit here during the day. The cave appeared dug out from within a large incline of dirt, barely authentically occurring. Quietly, Wyatt took hesitant steps down to the cave, climbing over the dead trees and leaf litter towards the cave's entrance.

Peeking in, he saw the cave was far deeper than expected, and even in broad daylight, it was dark inside, and he could see little. Faint noises came from within.

God damn, Carter was right, he thought. Although a part of him wondered if it was not in fact a real monster's home he was about to wander into. He hoped not.

Wyatt drew the gun hanging from his belt, and held it up in front of him ready for whomever may or may not be Joe. Cautiously, he took further steps into the darkness, gently placing his boots on the ground to minimise his sound.

Through the echoed silence, a slow click came from within the cave. The unmistakable sound of a six-round revolver, being cocked steadily. Each cog of the hammer bounced throughout the walls.

"Please, leave," implored a cautious, quiet voice bouncing within the walls of the cave, "I don't mean no harm," it continued. The voice was wheezy, tired, and afraid.

"Joe?" Wyatt replied to the echo, halting his movement with his gun held out ahead.

"Joe?" the voice replied quietly, "Joe..." it tailed off, Then: "Wyatt?" The voice had perked up, but was still hoarse.

Hardly able to believe what he was hearing, Wyatt replied sweet and brightened "Yeah, Joe, it's me." The cave was too dark to find a figure, but Wyatt knew that voice, and he smiled.

No further reply was heard, but the sound of movement continued, and the slowing clicking of a revolver's hammer gave its final snap into place, the metallic noise closer than before. Wyatt heard slow, heavy footsteps through the cave, each one more prominent than the last, until finally they stopped, and heavy, deep breathing was heard not far from Wyatt's face. In the murky darkness, Wyatt could just make out the silhouette of a large, humanoid bear towering over him, its chest caving in and puffing out with every coarse, deep breath.

Wyatt held still and felt the sudden tension of a cold gun barrel pressed between his eyes. Frozen, fearful, and blind, he allowed it to stay.

"What brings you to my woods, Wyatt?" growled the voice, still sounding afraid, and pushing the gun further into Wyatt's skin, "three years late." The voice became angry, and small drops of spin his Wyatt's face.

"Joe, come on," Wyatt said shaking, his voice wobbling. The gun released pressure from Wyatt's head and dropped. Joe's silhouette stayed prominent before him.

"I ain't got no energy," Joe said, breathy and exasperated, "where the fuck you bin'?" Wyatt knew it was time for this, but couldn't help but not be ready. His lips trembled having to look his brother in the eyes, unable to tell in the dark whether Joe was afraid, angry, or exhausted.

"Waiting for you," he said slowly and eerily, "could you not find me?"

The sounds of Joe calming down and backing off thumped over to a far corner of the cave. With a flash of light, and a subsequent earthy glow, Joe struck a match, before lighting a lantern, and revealing his face to Wyatt. After 3 years of only seeing it in posters, Wyatt's jaw loosened, as he tried to stop it from dropping. Joe was a mess. His hair was long, his beard was scruffy, his hat floppy and covered in shards of broken leaves, his face was a dirt-covered mask, showing only his exhausted eyes peering through the disguise. Joe was wearing the same clothes he'd worn on the last day Wyatt had saw him, now affected by time. The same coat and shirt but ripped in places, various small animal pelts hanging from his belt, and a generous application of mud scattered from head to toe.

The glow of the lantern softly lit up the ground of the cave. It was almost completely covered in the scattered bones of small animals, twigs, and dead leaves. The walls were decorated with childish drawings and paintings, fashioned from wonky scratches, chalk what might have been old, dried blood. Wyatt's eyes snuck peeks at the cave's artwork, knowingly watched by Joe's stare. They were mostly of people, two people, with matching hats. They seemed to be the two main characters in all of the sketches, appearing in some next to groups of other stick-men, or next to animals, or by a campfire.

"Is that us?" Wyatt asked carefully, pointing to the wall where bunches of similar carved-in drawings were etched.

"Could've been," Joe said bluntly after a short pause, not breaking his stare from behind the lantern.

"Could be again," Wyatt responded calmly, but eagerly, playing on Joe's yearning for the past as an opportunity to get him back on side. Wyatt's awkward smile didn't faze Joe, he just continued to stare, only his eyes were visible in the low light behind his camouflaged face.

"Thirsty," Joe said, completely ignoring Wyatt's response. Joe placed the lantern on the ground and abruptly stormed past Wyatt to the cave's exit. Confused and a little annoyed, Wyatt followed intently.

The still midday sun came as a shock to Wyatt after his eyes had adjusted to the cave. He was so surprised at how little light actually made its way into the cave, that he'd all but forgotten the sun was out. Joe was further out than Wyatt, already making his way deeper into the forest without looking, and with no regard for whether Wyatt was following him. As Joe ventured further into the trees, he became more elusive in Wyatt's line of vision, and so Wyatt jogged after him.

Doing his best to navigate through the bosky coppice in search of Joe, Wyatt emerged into a small glade, enclosed by thicker parts of the forest. The grass was greener, and flowers grew inside. Running through its centre, was a clean stretch of water, shimmering with the fish's scales that reflected the sunlight. Joe was on his knees over the other side, bent over and drinking from the stream with cupped hands. Just to his side, was a small, young deer drinking from the same stream with him, just a couple of feet away, as though it were completely accustomed and comfortable with Joe being near it.

Wyatt laid his feet down gently, taking steps closer to the stream, trying not to snap twigs or brush the ground. He removed his hat, and kept his eyes locked on the doe, trying not to startle it as he got closer, and trying to blend in with the sound of tranquility around.

Just as he brushed past a small weed with his shin, it pinged back and lightly tapped another, breaking the silence with the tiniest slap. The deer's head shot up, clocking Wyatt standing ahead of him sheepishly, and it bolted back into the forest and out of sight. Joe lifted his body and watched as the doe ran, before turning to Wyatt and shooting him an icy, judgmental expression.

"Sorry," Wyatt whispered, with the same sheepish look on his face. Without further concern for the out-of-sight wildlife, Wyatt stomped to the stream and sat on a log opposite Joe with the water flowing between them.

"What?" Joe teased, as their eyes were lined up.

"I need your help," Wyatt said, without breaking the unintentional staring contest that seemed to be taking place, with scrutinous undertones, and a little competition in the backs of their minds.

"So?" Joe asked monotonously.

"So, help?" Wyatt retorted, trying to hold on to his older brother authority, despite Joe's disinterest.

"No," Joe cupped his hands and lowered his head back down to the stream to drink, concluding their intense staring.

"Joe, let me explain," Wyatt insisted. "There's a man in Rockriver, a bad man, and he's-" Joe interrupted Wyatt by splashing his hand down into the water, soaking his arm and face.

"I ain't goin' back," Joe hissed with his wet arm pointed at Wyatt.

"No, no," Wyatt waved his arms ahead of him trying to calm Joe's sudden temper, "I ain't sayin' that."

"Good," Joe began to settle again, "I hate it there."

Finally, some words, Wyatt thought. "You don't ever have to go back."

"They called me *Big* Joe, I ain't even that big," Joe muttered, "ain't no one call me Big Joe out here."

"Well, let me finish then," Wyatt continued, "there's a man in Rockriver, a bad man-" Wyatt paused to test if Joe would react again, but he stayed calm.

"Bad man in Rockriver, okay," Joe nodded along, like a sulking toddler being read a nursery rhyme.

"He's given me the money we need to get that ranch," Wyatt smiled. Joe perked up and his eyes widened. He cracked a tiny smile before hiding it again.

"The Ranch," he said with a smirk and beaming eyes.

"That's right, but not so fast," Wyatt tried to reign Joe's oncoming excitement in so he could finish, "the problem is that I have to pay him back too much." He looked at Joe hesitantly, hoping Joe would not be too fazed.

"So, you need help payin'? I ain't got nothin', Wyatt," Joe frowned.

"No," Wyatt smirked, "I need your help in case he catches us runnin'." Joe froze a little and stared down at the stream, contemplating the many outcomes of Wyatt's situation, like a child trying to build a puzzle in his mind. On the one hand, Joe could be a cowboy again, a life he missed but did not have the capacity to see was damaging. On the other, he had grown quite fond of the forest. But, he too did miss his brother. And on the other hand again, he didn't much miss Rockriver and was scared to even think of it again. *Too much, too much,* he thought, and shook his head to get the difficult thoughts away. He paused, then smiled at the stream and leaned forward again to take another drink.

Wyatt watched Joe gulping, trying to think of something else to say. In the calm glade, just as Wyatt opened his mouth and took a small breath to speak, a large group of birds quickly scattered out of the trees above them, shaking the branches and flittering away. Wyatt looked up startled, and looked back down to see Joe staring up too. With haste, Joe stood and stumbled, swiftly turning and jogging back into the forest like a startled animal.

"Joe, wait!" Wyatt shouted, chasing after him. His foot splashed in the stream as he failed to jump it entirely. Looking behind him, he thought *what's Joe scared of?* Calling out "Joe, wait!" he took off running through the trees again, rapidly chasing glimpses of Joe ahead of him whilst tree trunks rushed past.

Joe dived over a fallen, thick tree, and laid down behind it, clinging to the ground. Wyatt, out of breath, caught up and climbed the log finding Joe laying there.

"Get down!" Joe hissed as he grasped Wyatt's shirt and pulled. Wyatt fell to the ground next to Joe like a rag-doll.

"What the hell, Joe?" Wyatt hissed back, demanding an answer for Joe's erratic behaviour, but receiving no response. But once noticing the fear on Joe's face, Wyatt turned his attention away and back to the forest around him. Joe wasn't worried about what Wyatt was saying, he was sweating, his mouth was open, and he looked like he was going to cry. Every few seconds or so, Joe quickly peeked over the top of the log, before collapsing back down again. *The hunt,* Wyatt thought with sudden realisation.

"We'll get it this time, boys!" came an aggressive voice from deep within the forest, ushered by the various sounds of other men laughing and chatting.

"Gettin' closer," Joe muttered quietly to himself. Again, he shot up, and sprinted further, abandoning the log. Reflexively, Wyatt's hand checked for his gun. Hesitating, he quickly followed Joe again. Another fallen tree was just ahead, and Joe tumbled over it for its cover.

"Got my gun," Wyatt panted, as he landed behind the second log next to Joe.

"Ain't no good," Joe said, as he peeked over the log, still in panic mode.

"But ain't this fun?" Wyatt pulled his lips back to show his teeth in the parody of a grin. The smile didn't reach his eyes. He adjusted his belt slightly in case he needed to quick-draw. Joe said nothing, and continued to press his body into the ground, trying to control his breathing, but failing.

"I hear somethin' up here!" a faint voice came from the trees.

"Footprints!" another voice bellowed. Joe looked around for an escape, gritting his teeth. The view was the same in every direction, and he couldn't tell where the voices were coming from.

"Down here!" another voice came from the other side. *We're surrounded,* Wyatt thought.

"Ready?" Wyatt winked at Joe, placing his hand on his gun and preparing to jump to his feet. Joe frowned and rolled his eyes, and pulled a dirty pistol from under one of the pelts attached to his jeans.

The crunching of leaves and twigs came closer to their log from every angle, and slowly, a handful of men poked their rifles through the trees and emerged one by one.

"*Sasquatch,*" hissed one of the men from the side.

There were only two in Wyatt's eye-line, facing them dead-on. *The rest must be behind us, we're protected by the log for now.* Wyatt threw Joe a prepared look. Joe understood. Still seated, Joe and Wyatt rapidly unveiled their pistols together, and shot ahead. One dead... then, Wyatt missed. The still living man was shocked, checking his torso to discover that he was unscathed. Letting out a mean snigger, he pointed his rifle to Wyatt's head again, but before he could pull the trigger, another bullet fired, and blood oozed from a little hole in the man's forehead. He stared unseeing as he dropped his rifle, before flopping forward into the leaves.

"Thanks," Wyatt whispered to Joe.

"Come on out, now," one of the voices sneered from behind them. There was fear in his voice, having not expected any gun-related counter-attack from 'Sasquatch.'

"Don't shoot!" Joe shouted, bringing the slow sound of footsteps to a sudden stop. Wyatt looked at him in horror. *Now, what the hell are you doing?* he thought. There was no telling what Joe might do next. Wyatt watched, heart sinking in his chest, as Joe slowly stood, with his arms in the air. The men slowed down with caution, but kept their rifles on Joe.

"Well, goddam, it's- it's a man," one of them said, as bewildered as if he'd really found a mythical creature. Joe counted. *Four,* he thought, *Wyatt was right, this will be fun.* Wyatt looked up at Joe, sighed, and stood up slowly as well. *Only four?* Wyatt thought, gently turning his head to Joe, who almost looked like he was smiling.

"Joe?" Wyatt whispered as quietly as he could with his arms raised up. Joe didn't reply, he just looked at the men ahead of him intently.

"Shut up!" the same man yelled as he waved his rifle at them.
Knowing any sudden movement would set off this man's finger on the trigger, Joe considered his next move. Slowly, he began to lower one of his raised hands but maintained eye contact with the gunman. Joe, instead of reaching for his gun, dropped suddenly down and crouched. The man, as Joe predicted, was startled by Joe's sudden drop, and a rifle bullet exploded from the chamber and flew right over Joe's head. Despite his heavy frame, Joe was fast, and he had drawn his weapon and shot upwards from the ground before the others could. With one finger on the trigger, and the other on the hammer, he fired three simultaneous bullets, darting his aim to the gunmen between each shot. Three of the four fell silent, and hit the ground.

"*Jesus!*" Wyatt yelled struggling to take it in. *Boy hasn't lost his touch!* "Just like old times," he chuckled, removing his hands from his ears.

The last man standing tried to hide his quiver as he watched Joe slowly rise to his feet again, gun still in hand. Joe's head blocked the sun as he began to tower over the hunter, and a menacing shadow engulfed him.

"Come on then, asshole!" the hunter yelled with feigned confidence, standing amongst the corpses of his friends. "Come on!" He felt his fear-induced sweat drip into his eyes as Joe took slow steps towards him. The hunter knew now, that as Joe closed the short distance between them, he had no intention of shooting him. Joe dropped his gun, and clenched his fists.

The hunter panicked as Joe approached, and pulled the trigger on his rifle. Nothing happening, it just clicked. Fueled by fear and adrenaline, and without thinking, he threw his rifle to the ground at Joe's feet, and began to hop in place and loosen his muscles, clicking his knuckles as he did.

"Come on, asshole!" the hunter continued, holding back any outward sign of fear. As he approached the hunter, Joe quickly jerked his hand forward and held back any impact. The hunter flinched, and looked up at Joe with embarrassment and desperation. And just as he began to think Joe's mockery was a sign of mercy, Joe jerked forwards again, and thumped his fist into the hunter's chest. For Joe, the punch was nothing, but for the hunter, it took every ounce of energy he had to stay standing. Having not expected this, Joe punched again, ramming his fist harder into the hunter's ribs. The hunter wobbled and stepped back upon impact, but against the odds, stayed standing. His eyes began to roll backwards and forwards as the images of unconsciousness and a waking nightmare flicked simultaneously in front of him. As he wobbled, another crunch hit his chest, cracking through his ribs and taking the air from his lungs, knocking him backwards again. He could barely stand. The snap of his ribs caving inwards was a pain he never imagined, triggering a deep breath inward which only filled his damaged lungs with more blood. As he gagged on his blood and coughed it up, the convulsions knocked him back further.

It took no more barraging. The hunter's own retching and pain forced him to fall. As he hit the ground, the impact on his back shot through and smarted in his chest. His heart was in pain, and failing. He couldn't breathe. But he could see.

The last thing the hunter saw was Joe looking down on him twitching and spitting blood. Joe had his gun in hand again, and with no further expression on his filthy face, aimed at the hunter's face, and pulled the trigger.

Damn you, Sasquatch, the hunter thought, and it was lights out.

"You should go now, Wyatt," Joe muttered, holstering his weapon. Wandering over to the bodies, he began searching their clothes and flopping them back down, removing trinkets, cigarettes, and any pocketed food they were carrying.

"Joe, really?" Wyatt sighed placatory, "I thought you liked this!"

"Leave," Joe replied, still looting the bodies.

"You don't remember what you said to me that last day in Rockriver?" Wyatt persisted. "You said you hated it and you wanted to be a *real* cowboy again. Well, this is our chance!"

"No, Wyatt, you always said that's bad!" Joe snapped, dropping a body as he stood and faced Wyatt, a trace of toddler-like outrage in his expression.

"Well dammit, Joe, maybe I miss it too!" Wyatt shouted, "maybe I took it for granted!"

"I miss it all, Wyatt, and you ain't never cared!" Joe exploded, stepping closer to Wyatt, "'cause you only care 'bout yourself and *Holy* Mary, and no Joe!" he whined, turning his back on his brother.

"Hell, Joe, I care, I just didn't see it none! Let's start over, let's take this asshole's money and burn the breeze!" Wyatt pleaded.

"No!" Joe shouted, staring Wyatt down, standing his ground. Wyatt belittled, softly nodded in defeat.

"Well then," he muttered, "S'pose I'll just go back to Mary and suffer under the bad man's control." He snuck a look at Joe to see if this parting shot had hit the mark. Joe appeared unaffected by Wyatt's new tactic, and turned away, heading back to his cave.

"Goodbye, Wyatt," Joe murmured under his breath as he walked away, trying not to look back.

"Joe!" *Goddam his ass!* thought Wyatt watching morosely as Joe disappeared back into the trees.

Shit. What now? Wyatt thought as he looked around. Nothing but forest, and no Joe. *Follow him, maybe? No, tried that, made him angry.* Though he had never tested the theory, Wyatt knew that he was no match for Joe, and now that Joe had a reason to direct his anger directly at Wyatt, he was humbled.

Sullenly and purposelessly, Wyatt wandered through the forest. A little lost, he didn't pass Joe's cave again, and instead found the edge of the forest about a hundred feet from where he'd left Banjo. A little exhausted and run down, Wyatt didn't fancy the walk, so whistled for Banjo in the distance to come to him and waited.

"Just you and me," he muttered to Banjo and patted his neck upon his arrival. Mounting up, he looked back at the forest again, tossing thoughts around his mind. *Return to Rockriver? Go after him again?*

Reluctantly, he headed back home, knowing Mary's fate should be the same as his. A slow, prolonged walk home, however. Wyatt needed time alone.

11: Henry

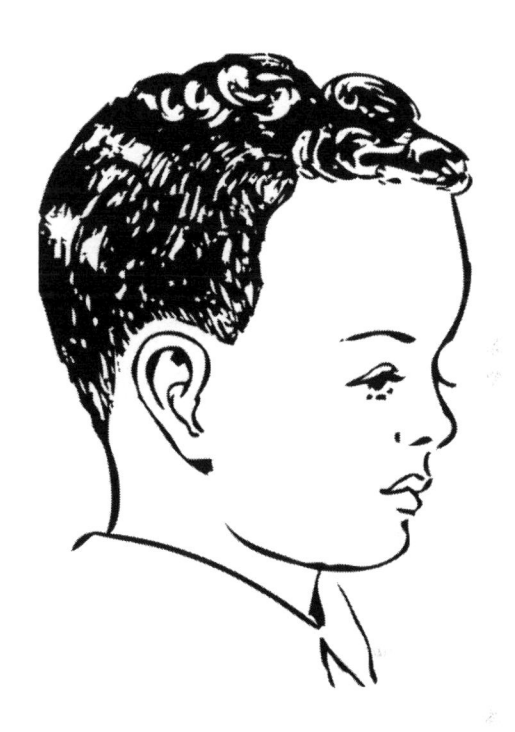

Carter & Smith Brewery, California, 1842

Through no fault of his own, Henry Carter was born to a strict and cruel father. At only seven years young, Henry spent most of his time in his father's office, within the only brewery in West California. Not much of a childhood was had prior to this, especially not since the violent death of his brother, Elmer Junior, when Henry was only five. For the most recent two years of his life, Henry was mostly alone, with the exception of the few times a day that Elmer Senior would burst into the office in a dizzy, rageful fit, that he'd take out physically on poor Henry.

It hadn't always been like this. Henry's father used to be a fairly loving man, behind his strict exterior. As a religious man, Elmer Carter Senior spitefully blamed God for the death of his first son. To Elmer, his son's death was not at all related to him being young and inexperienced in the hands of heavy, dangerous machinery. Since that day, Elmer became angry, feeling as though he'd wasted his time praising and believing in a God that took his first son.

Henry treasured his alone time in the office, playing quietly with Elmer Junior's model horses that had now become his own. Although it was peaceful, every second was another closer to the next inevitable outburst from his father. Already sporting cuts and bruises, Henry waited ignorantly for his next beratement or beating. Out of sight, out of mind.

"Henry!" a deep voice bellowed from the other side of the door. Henry's ears shot up and he dropped his toy horse onto the panelled wood floor. The door swung open to reveal his father, Elmer, with a wet stain down the front of his shirt. He had an empty glass in his hand, and a mean, scrunched-up look on his sweaty, panting face.

Before Henry had a chance to speak through his choked up shock, the glass in Elmer's hand came smashing down onto the carpet next to Henry's feet, scattering glass throughout the room, and pinching Henry's skin. Elmer walked slowly closer to Henry, whilst he shuffled back, cowering further into the wall.

"You know what this is, boy?" Elmer sneered, pointing at his sodden chest. Henry cowered more, opened his mouth but unable to get a word out. It was just short, sharp breathing. "Answer me, boy!" Elmer yelled and slammed his fist at the wall beside them both, shaking the office.

"I don't know," Henry whimpered as he started to cry, and shielded his face under his hand. Elmer knelt down before Henry and gritted his teeth, starting quiet, and raising into another scream.

"This here's the remnants of the last *God* damn drink in this factory!" he slammed his fist against the wall again, closer to Henry's head. A factory-uniformed figure unknown to Henry stood in the doorway behind his father, and he caught a glimpse of eyes that matched his own. They were sunken, lifeless, and passionless. Elmer's word-weary clerk held his gaze on Henry, and he slowly closed the door, leaving Henry and his father alone.

Where is mother? Henry thought to himself, as he felt his tears tickle his cheeks. Elmer reached out and grabbed Henry by the scruff of his shirt, pulling him closer. Henry's chest jolted forward towards his father, slinging his head back, but still in line with his father's yellow, mocking stare which pierced into Henry's soul.

Elmer scoffed. Letting go, he threw Henry to the floor, before stepping back and nearly stumbling into his desk with a wobble. Sitting unsteadily on the desk, he watched Henry, who was quietly sobbing into his arms in a ball against the wall.

"Look at you," he spat, "ain't nothing on Junior." He turned to his desk, reached over it with a leg in the air, and pulled a sealed bottle of whiskey from the other side.

Damn liar, Henry thought, knowing these beatings had nothing to do with any drink.

"If you hadn't left one of your damn horses for me to trip on, I'd have never had to open this," Elmer said, cracking the top and taking a gulp. "I were savin' this'n," he wiped his mouth, and stumbled over to Henry again. "Do you want to know what for?" he said, his crooked smile inches from Henry's face with hot, boozy air blowing into it.

Elmer pulled back, bolted forward and fired a fist square into Henry's small skull, tripping to the side and falling as he did. Henry yelped in pain, sobbing, and cupping his crown where the pain was throbbing. With a crash, his father hit the floor, the whiskey bottle hanging out of his stretched arm, dripping onto the wood. Nearly passing out, wheezing, he reached for the bottle. With a slurred mutter, he spoke slowly as he lay struggling to move.

"I were savin' it for Junior," a small tear trickled down the side of his face and into the wood, "for when he became a man," he rolled his head on the floor to see Henry again. "Do you hear me, boy?" he slurred, watching Henry sit curled in a ball through a swirling haze. Elmer laid his head back again and stared at the ceiling defeated. For a moment, the office fell silent, but Henry was still too afraid to uncurl. He was shaking, questioning whether his father was just sleeping or quietly brewing his next outburst.

In a feat of bravery, Henry lifted his head in the silence, and listened to his father's strained breathing. He saw him lying, arms and legs outstretched, the half empty bottle beside him, a stain where it had leaked and soaked into the floor. Elmer just stared through the space above him, blinking slowly.

"It should've been you," Elmer croaked through his slow panting. Henry's eyes widened as he heard, uncurled, and inched closer to his father to hear better.

"He would've been the good one," Elmer continued, "God took my son, and the Devil left me with the scraps. That's you, Henry," his eyes closed but his breathing continued. Henry's sniffling in fear became that of more sadness, as his innocent ears heard his father's true feelings, "I got nothin' left," Elmer's wheezing turned into a heavy snore.

"Father?" Henry hesitated, checking to see if this was all over. He got no response, other than a choked-up snore and a sense of worthlessness. Henry stood up slowly and wiped his head to check for blood.

Nothing this time, he thought, before waddling over to Elmer's sleeping pile of stink. This wasn't a scenario unknown to Henry; this had happened before. He approached and removed his own shirt before gently lifting Elmer's head to place his scrunched-up shirt under it. Gently laying his father's head back down, so as to not wake him, Henry picked up the dripping bottle and landed it on the desk.

Henry tried the door, but it had been locked. Disappointed, he sat back down by the wall, shirtless, and getting colder. With only his sleeping father for company, he picked up the toy horse again. Elmer Junior had left nothing but the toys, no pictures, no letters, Elmer Junior was just a child like him, with no legacy.

"If I have a son, I'll name him after you," Henry muttered, looking into the toy horse's face, "I won't never hurt you, Junior," he continued, "I'm gon' become a good man, not like father," Henry's eyes began to twitch again, with only a toy horse to remember his brother by, "I hope you see me, Junior, I'll make you proud," his muttering becoming more stuttered, choking and sniffing between his words. "They're gonna remember us as important men, doin' God's work."

Henry pressed his back into the wall, struggling to get comfortable, holding his horse to his chest. Elmer stayed still, snoring loudly over the sounds of the factory machines in the adjoining rooms. Henry was spent and his thoughts ran awry. He gazed at his father, wondering what would happen next, and how he could leave, and if his mother only knew.

He reached in his pocket and held a tiny Bible. He didn't know where it came from, only that he found it on the factory floor one day. The writing was small, but Henry had been taught by rich parents to read at a young age. He'd read the Bible a multitude of times since finding it, so much so that it had become a comfort and an escape from reality. He laid his horse down, and opened the book again. Trying to ignore his father in the corner of his eye, he focused on the book and took it in once again, mouthing the words slowly as he did.

"Proverbs 28:7," Henry mumbled, "whoever keeps the law is a wise son: but he that is a companion of riotous men shames his father." He had trouble understanding this one. He skipped over to Proverbs 28:13.

"Whoever conceals their sins does not prosper, but the one who confesses and renounces them finds mercy." He looked at his father, still asleep, and wondered if this proverb could be the reason for his father's suffering.

"Proverbs 28:19. The one who works his land will have plenty of food, but whoever chases fantasies will have his fill of poverty." *Plenty of land,* Henry thought, and misinterpreted.

"Proverbs 28:25. A greedy man stirs up strife, but he who trusts in the Lord will prosper." *Trust in the Lord,* Henry thought, unaware of strife's definition.

The only book you need, his father used to say. Although at this moment, Henry had trouble believing it. As a child, it was hard to see his father negatively, despite his actions. Henry didn't know any different anymore. However, he found a comforting home in the book and its stories. Many times, he had rested in the office, many times with the sleeping lump that was his father, and read page after page, recovering from his cuts and bruises. There were examples of good men and bad men, good deeds and bad deeds, in black and white for a child to understand. The issue for Henry was that that he had nobody to teach him who was good, and who was bad.

12: A Motivator Calls

The Wilson homestead, the outskirts of Rockriver, California, February, 1880

As the sun crept over, the birds' songs brought in the early morning. Bright yellow light lit up the Wilsons' kitchen, leaving the bright shapes of the windows pasted on the wall. Mary sat up by the fire, her arms crossed, and her legs outstretched, facing the front door, waiting patiently for Wyatt to return home.

Her eyes glanced up when she heard the slow sounds of a horses' hooves approaching the front door. It was unclear, but somebody murmured to the horse. It was him. The door crept open, but the effort to silence its creaking only prolonged it.

"You can't take him back to the livery?" Mary quipped, before Wyatt had even revealed himself. The door stopped moving halfway, Wyatt sighed from the other side and emerged, with his head held low.

"Mary," he uttered, still looking down.

"It's been three days," she continued despite his disinterest, "where were you?" she bit back in anger, and although Wyatt wouldn't look, he felt that, knowing her well enough to envision her angry face. Taking a deep breath, he looked up. His face hit the light coming through the window, and revealed the redness of his cheeks, and the residue of tears from his journey. Mary's arms unfolded as she became concerned. *Has something happened?* she thought, thinking only of her husband.

"I found him," Wyatt held back the tears, and his voice was quiet and hoarse, "J- Joe," his head fell again, to hide his persistent tears. Mary's concern changed, as she put the pieces together. She crept up to Wyatt at the doorway, and tilted her head below his to lift his eyes back into hers.

"You took the deal?" she whispered, unshaken by his mood. Wyatt was silent, and just sniffled back. "Did you take the deal?" she said louder. "Answer me, Wyatt!" she shouted through the silence into his face.

"Yes," Wyatt responded quickly, trying to maintain his masculinity with a tight gaze. Mary turned away, stopped and slowed her breathing, "Mary?" Wyatt said quietly, to no response, "Holy Mary?" he said with a forced smirk. Mary swung back around, and her open palm struck Wyatt's clammy cheek, batting his head to the side.

"Don't you talk to me like that, Wyatt!" she held her hand in place and pointed an inch from his face, shaking her arm in time with her yelling, "Don't you ever even think you can talk to me like that again!" Mary began to cry, spitting her words through her pain, "I trusted you, Wyatt, and now look what you done, all for yourself, you don't never think about me, about us!" she backed away, and stumbled back into her chair by the fire.

"Mary, I-" Wyatt closed the door and wandered closer to her.

"Stay!" her eyes shot back to his, and her arm lifted again with a finger outstretched, "don't come one step closer I swear, Wyatt!" Her crying made her sentences difficult.

"He's my brother, Mary, I had to," Wyatt pleaded, cautiously taking a couple of steps closer, "he's all I got."

Mary's crying became more apathetic. "All you got?" she gazed at him through her tear-stained eyes. Wyatt quietly scoffed, and dropped his hands in defeat.

"Well not like that, Mary, damn!" he sighed.

"No, Wyatt, like that!" she insisted, "you're always actin' like I don't even exist, like I don't matter, you have put us in danger, in another man's debt!"

"Mary, I did this for you too!"

"Like hell! You did this for yourself!" she yelled, "well guess what, you're on your own now, enjoy your money, enjoy your family, I ain't cookin', I ain't cleanin', who's gon' do that now?" She paused briefly, staring intently waiting for Wyatt's reply. He said nothing. "Yeah," she continued with a sarcastic smile, "the Devil gon' be doin' it, 'cause Carter's gon' *kill* you, when he finds out we can't pay him back!"

"Please, Mary," Wyatt sighed, becoming impatient.

"No," Mary waved her hand ahead of her, "don't talk, don't even-," She was interrupted by a knock on the door catching Wyatt's attention. Déjà vu. Carter.

"Wyatt?" An all too familiar voice came from the other side of the door. "Holy Mary?" The sardonic timbre was unmistakable, and Wyatt turned back to Mary with panic in his eyes and his breathing harsh. Silence filled the room, and Wyatt and Mary heard one another's hearts, still rushed with emotion.

"Mary!" Wyatt whispered as quietly as he could, staring desperately for support. He suppressed his breathing, and sweat began to drip from his forehead. Although Mary was upset, the concern for their well-being was still shared. Mary lifted a finger to her lips. *Shhh!* Wyatt gave her a tiny nod and held his pose, finding a small amount of comfort in her confidence.

"Look, I heard you as I was comin' down the path," Carter continued outside, "but don't trouble yourselves." Confused, Wyatt and Mary stayed as still as they could, trusting in each other's silence. "Just a friendly reminder," Carter continued, "it's thirty-five tomorrow, I'll be round in the mornin'." The sound of Carter's coat hit the door as he turned, announcing his departure.

"Stop him!" Mary whispered harshly, gesturing at Wyatt frantically, "get us out of this!" Wyatt looked back and forth with a lost look in his eyes, panicking and not knowing where to start. He ran to the door and quickly swung it open to see Carter, walking towards Al and Billy who were unhitching their horses.

"Carter, wait!" Wyatt reached out, hesitated, then stepped back suddenly as Carter swung back around. He had that signature smirk on his face.

"So, you are home?" Carter asked boldly.

"Listen, Carter," Wyatt panted, "thirty-five a week, I just, I can't." His panic and desperation tripped up his words.

"No excuses, Wyatt, you signed," Carter interrupted with a chuckle, "find it by tomorrow and there'll be no problem, see?" He made sure his holster was visible to Wyatt, subtly pushing his long coat aside. Carter turned back around and began to walk. Wyatt became restless, and panicked.

"Asshole!" Wyatt shouted, stopping Carter dead in his tracks, still facing away. "You stiffed me, you son of a bitch!"

Carter remained unresponsive, making Wyatt shift uncomfortably in his doorway, unsettled by the wind whistling through the silence between his words.

Feining confidence, and hoping to call his bluff, he continued "get back here, Carter!" Another couple of loaded seconds, then Carter whipped back around and marched quickly to Wyatt. Before stumbling back could do Wyatt any good, Carter's frown grew stronger, and angrier, and he swung his fist into Wyatt's jaw.

"Don't talk, boy!" Carter screamed at Wyatt's dropped head, "you owe me $5,000, boy, and you are gon' pay it the way I want!" As Wyatt's head began to lift, Carter struck him again, knocking his head back down, this time letting the door slam behind him, shutting the two of them outside. Wyatt held his head low, and used his tongue to check for any missing teeth. He was fine. Taking a deep breath, he shot up, and with his good hand, cracked a fist right between Carter's eyes, knocking him backwards. It had been a while, but Wyatt hadn't missed the pain a man's nose can inflict on your hand. He shook his hand like it was covered in bugs and held his wrist in agony.

Carter ran his finger through his moustache and found it stained with his own blood. His breathing deepened, his eyebrows lowered, and his nose scrunched up like a petulant child.

"Oh, you done it now, boy," Carter said quietly, before once again leaning forward and charging for Wyatt. Before he got much closer, he was abruptly intercepted, by a stranger gently grabbing Carter's coat. *Where did he come from?* Carter and Wyatt thought simultaneously, unbeknownst to each other. The man stood with his arm stretched out to Carter, and a frightened, innocent look in his eyes.

"Fellas," the man spoke, moving one of his arms to Wyatt, standing between them. He adjusted the satchel that hung from his shoulder before lifting his arm again, "now, now," the man continued, watching Wyatt and Carter calm down upon being interrupted. It was Seamus, Wyatt's neighbour, passing through on his way home.

God dammit, Seamus, Wyatt thought, *of all the times you decide to come by, you come by now.* "Can I help you?" Wyatt panted, still holding his wrist and hand, exhausted and somewhat annoyed by the stranger's unannounced arrival. Seamus nodded with his eyes fixed on Wyatt. Quickly, he opened a satchel at his side and rummaged around. At last, he pulled a single letter from his bag and lifted it above him with a proud smile. Seeing Carter's frown, his smile was shot down.

"First day in Rockriver?" Carter rolled his eyes, and turned to wander to his horse, disappointed by the stranger being just another of his unfortunate clients. Before mounting, Carter pushed his hat down to cast a shadow on his nose, "I'll see you tomorrow, Wyatt! Hyaa!" He whipped the reins and kicked, riding off into the sunrise, with Al and Billy following at a respectful distance.

Seamus, startled, shakily turned to Wyatt.

"Sorry to interrupt, Wyatt," he stuttered quietly, like a scared mouse, "I picked up your post for you." He held out the letter to Wyatt as his arm quivered. "I were just on my way home," he continued shakily, "good timing, huh?" he smiled awkwardly.

"Thank you," Wyatt sighed, snatching the letter from Seamus, holding his wrist to his chest, and retiring back indoors without so much as a goodbye.

"Well, goodbye, Wyatt!" Seamus called out, before Wyatt reached his door, but Wyatt didn't respond and continued to walk away, leaving Seamus outdoors.

"Mature," Mary muttered, as Wyatt waddled back inside. She clocked the letter, and lifted her eyebrows to peek afar, "a letter? We never get letters," she said confused. As was usually the way, a boring life means a letter can change a mood. Their spite for each other now put aside, a mutual interest persisted.

"I know, it's strange," Wyatt said as he concentrated intently on the envelope's seal, clawing his dry fingertips at it trying to catch an opening. It wasn't especially neatly sealed, but it was definitely securely sealed, with ample amounts of string and a mess of dried wax. He found a corner to rip, and carefully split the envelope. With an inkling of what was to come, judging by its presentation, Wyatt slid the letter out. Messy handwriting.

"Shit," Wyatt said and slowly blinked, before reading aloud. Fighting through the spelling mistakes and ink blotches, Wyatt heard Joe's voice coming from the spidery, crooked words on the page.

Dear Wyatt,
I have thought about what you said, but you was already gone when I tried to stop you.
Do you promise that we are gon be okay? I hope you're right, you're always right, Wyatt.
I still wan be like you, I wan be a real cowboy, and stick it to that man you was talkin bout. Carter?
Anyway, I changed my mind, I wan come with you and Miss Mary, and help you on your ranch.
By the way, Wyatt, you ain't got to worry bout Carter no more. I have helped you. We got the upper hand, there ain't no way he's gon be the boss once he's sees what I done.
I want to show you what I done that's gon get you out of this mess.

Meet me at the old factory south of the river bank we used to camp at. You're gon love this.
Sincerely yours,
Joe.

"What in God's name have you started?" Mary was almost speechless. Wyatt's face revealed itself from behind the letter, his eyes was tormented, and terrified. For no one could predict any more what Big Joe was capable of. Mary frantically began moving. She grabbed a suitcase from the bedroom and started to empty the cupboard, spilling tins of food into the case. Pots, pans, and cutlery. She stumbled back to the bedroom and Wyatt heard her pulling drawers open and stuffing clothes in with the food.

"Mary?!" Wyatt shouted through the wall.

"You have to go," Mary came back through, with clothes spilling from the suitcase shoving it into Wyatt, "you have to run, hide, and find this goddamn *idiot* before he makes things worse."

"But the money, Mary..." Wyatt shrugged, gently placing the suitcase down.

"You let me handle that, my sweet." She placed a hand on Wyatt's shoulder, and for a moment Wyatt recognised the loving look in her eyes, "now get lost before I kick you out, asshole." She joked through the fear, with an ounce of sincerity.

"Mary-" Wyatt began, not wanting to take the luggage or leave.

"No," Mary interrupted. She brushed herself down and lifted a hat from the suitcase, sporting a light pink feather. She placed it on her head and took a deep breath. "I'll try and handle things here. You handle your god damn brother, and *fix* this."

13: Bad Luck

The abandoned Carter & Smith Brewery, California, one day later, 1880

The brewery had been closed for years, closed before Wyatt even arrived in California. It took Wyatt until this day to question why Carter would close one brewery, only to open another within the same few miles. Perhaps he just wanted something for his own, instead of sitting in his father's shadow. *Pathetic,* Wyatt thought.

The metal door under the building's scaffolding was a smidge open, with a broken lock clearly smashed by force. The unkept dirt and random tufts of grass around the door were kicked up, showing signs of a struggle. *Not good,* Wyatt continued his inner monologue.

Wyatt's heart began racing as his hand slowly reached out for the door, feeling each pump of blood through his body, hearing the thumping pulsing in his ears, get faster the closer he got.

When his fingertips touched the door, it was cold. *How long has he been here?* he wondered, expecting to have been met with warmth. He pushed the door open, to behold a vast, cold, empty room. The ceilings were high, and the floor was endless. Every machine, wall, and room that had once graced the building were ripped from its corpse.

There, in the centre of the room stood the distant frame of Joe, facing away from the door, staring down at something hidden by his large frame. He was still far, but Wyatt could swear he heard quiet talking, or muttering. *Is he talking to me? Himself?* Wyatt tip-toed into the room.

"Joe?" Wyatt said quietly, yet it echoed. His gentle call had repeated louder and louder as it bounced around the chamber-like room. Joe spun around with a smile.

"You made it!" Joe announced gleefully. There was something wrong, Wyatt could feel it. An abandoned building, the letter, Joe…

Wyatt was skeptical, but continued to take cautious steps towards Joe.

"W-what's goin' on, buddy?" Wyatt asked as he crept closer, but still too far to see what was happening behind Joe. Joe just smiled. That is when Wyatt noticed a dirty beaten-up pistol in Joe's hand and halted.

"Oh, this ain't for you, Wyatt," Joe said, clocking Wyatt's concern. Joe moved aside to reveal what he was hiding. His smile was wide and unsettling, and his eyes were crooked, "it's for her." He waved his hand as he stepped aside, presenting a woman sat on a chair. Strange and unexpected to say the least, but Wyatt thought it could be nothing. Upon further inspection, Wyatt could see that the woman was gagged, her hands were tied behind her back, her feet were bound at the base of the chair, and her tears were spilling down her face as the faint muffled sounds of desperation begged to be let out. Wyatt froze.

"Joe," Wyatt whispered hoarsely through a dry mouth, "tell me that ain't Miss Molly…" *Molly, Molly,* echoed around the room. Wyatt's chest pounded as he took in the full brevity of this situation. *Christ, Joe!*

Wyatt's brain tried to unpick the options. Setting her free would alert Carter and get everyone killed. Killing her could get everyone killed. And every second that passed, Molly filled the silence with her masked begging and gagged screaming, tears streaming down her floral dress. *Shut up!* thought Wyatt, *shut up!*

"It's good, huh, Wyatt?" Joe beamed and settled his gun in both hands, fiddling with it whilst he waited on Wyatt's approval. Wyatt stayed still, a fight or flight stance at the ready.

"No," Wyatt said hushed but sharply. Joe huffed, looked back at Molly and let the weight on the gun pull his arm back to his side. With another sigh, he left Molly and stomped over the length of the factory floor to Wyatt.

"You're not gettin' it, Wyatt, let me tell you," Joe muttered approaching Wyatt with heavy footfalls, he looked behind to make sure that Molly was out of ear shot.

"You gon' kill this girl, Joe?" Wyatt whispered, praying that Joe was still thinking somewhat logically.

"No, Wyatt, 'course not," Joe stated quietly, sighing with exasperation. "This is how we win!" His excitement fought with his attempts to keep quiet.

"Win what?!" Wyatt whispered holding back a bellow, still unsure of what he could do to help.

"It's that bad man's sister!" Joe smiled, pointing over at Molly, whose eyes begged for mercy in the distance.

"I know that!" hissed Wyatt, nudging Joe's stomach, and gritting his teeth, thickness and emphasis in his drawl. *Enough of this,* he thought. He pushed Joe aside and began marching to Molly.

"Wyatt, no!" Joe shouted after him. Wyatt stopped and turned, pointing his finger at Joe as he stood between him and Molly.

"You cannot do this, Joe, do you understand?" he said sternly, assuming the role of Joe's superior, before turning again and continuing towards Joe's hostage.

"Wyatt, we're cowboys, ain't no one mess with cowboys!" Joe pleaded, watching Wyatt get closer to Molly.

"We *ain't* cowboys no more, Joe, you understand?" he turned again, holding Joe's gaze, "cowboys, *bad,*" Wyatt asserted, speaking to Joe like he was a dog.

"But, Wyatt, you said, just like old times!" Joe persisted, frustrated at Wyatt's indifference. Wyatt ignored him, and approached Molly, "Wyatt!" whined Joe, now behind him.

"It's gon' be okay, ma'am," Wyatt muttered as he arrived at Molly's chair, immediately getting to work on the ropes around her feet. Joe huffed and watched, with his gun just resting on one finger swinging with each step. Like a tantrum, he watched his feet kick as he walked, looking down as he frowned. He had a tough decision to make, he didn't want to upset Wyatt. He looked up and sighed again, his eyes following Wyatt over by Molly's chair.

"What you doin', Wyatt? Stop!" he whined.

Wyatt's eyes met Molly's as he knelt to help her. She was terrified. Her sweat suffocated the rope in her mouth, and her cheeks were almost bleeding from the beating they'd had from her tears. Drool had dripped down her chin, and she spat through her teeth with each quick breath she exhaled. He held his eyes on hers, noticing the rope tied around her neck, attaching it to the backrest of the chair. He began loosening the grip on her neck, remembering how painful it could be. Molly's breathing sped up as he loosened it, and Wyatt felt her anger shift as the enhanced speed of her breath hit his face. She kept her gaze on Wyatt as her brow furrowed, and he then he realised too late what he'd done.

Molly bolted her head forward, colliding it with Wyatt's and knocking him backwards with a smack as he flopped to the ground. Frantically, she shook at the last rope around her arms and waist, staring at Wyatt's unconscious body.

"Wyatt!" Joe screamed, and the echo crashed off the walls. He sprung into motion, and headed in Molly's direction. Every leap Joe took shook the building as he hit the floor. Molly panicked, shaking and wriggling at the rope, darting her eyes up and down seeing Joe quickly getting closer.

"My brother! My brother!" Close up, Molly could see the animalistic rage in his face. Spit was dripping from his mouth as he yelled, his eyes barely showing under his furrowed forehead.

"My brother! My brother!" Hopping over Wyatt's prone body, he threw his pistol down and lifted both of his arms above him like a gorilla, and Molly stopped her struggling seeing Joe's arms come down in his last steps from her.

Like the ceiling was falling, Joe's fists slammed into Molly's shoulders. The chair beneath her shattered and splintered as she crashed through it and onto the floor. *I'm free,* she thought with a glimmer of hope, though aching pain shot through her delicate body. *There!* she caught a glimpse of Joe's abandoned gun on the floor. Not able to stand, she scrambled on her hands and knees and swiftly slipped between Joe's legs as he tried to grab at her. *Got it!* she smiled to herself as she grasped the pistol. Rolling onto her back, and pointing true, she watched Joe barrel towards her again. Closing one eye, she pulled back the hammer, and focused on Joe's chest. Closing her other eye, she gritted her teeth, and prayed she was strong enough to pull the trigger.

Bang! A moment of silence fell across the empty room, following the intense ringing and echo of the gunshot in Molly's ears. The room once filled with the deafening sounds of anger had been immediately silenced.

Expecting to have been mauled by now, she opened an eye, and peeked ahead of her again. There stood Joe, weakened, touching the small circle of blood that had began to appear on his heart. He tasted it. *What the hell?!* Molly panicked, *why isn't he dead? What did I do wrong?!*

"You shot me…" Joe slurred quietly, looking innocently at Molly, laying on her back with the gun still pointed at him, almost showing a sense of sympathy, "You shot me!" Joe got louder, as he began to stagger over to Molly. His face was red, and veiny, and his eyes began to turn bloodshot.

Bang! Bang! Molly panicked as he edged closer, and shot twice again. She shuffled backwards with the gun outstretched, crying and whimpering, as Joe remained unaffected by the gunshots, only enraged further. He lifted his arms again, higher, and tenser. She didn't want to see. Molly curled into a ball and scrunched her eyes, just as Joe's giant hands whooshed through the air and smashed into Molly again. And again. Molly's mind became foggy and her body unravelled. She could feel Joe's hands, but each time he thumped her, she felt it less. Joe dropped to his knees, with Molly between his legs, and with one hand at a time he pummeled into Molly's once beautiful face. Between each smack, Molly could recognise the foggy vision of Joe's sweaty, coarse face, which with each hit, became fainter, and fainter. And each hit became quieter, and quieter. Until nothing. Somewhere between fear and nirvana, Molly fell silent.

Joe stopped, and remained sat on Molly's abdomen, with darkened blood dripping from his brick-like fists. He stared menacingly at the mangled crater that was once an innocent young face. Then it set in: he was shot. He lifted himself from her, feeling the burning in his chest as he crawled to Wyatt.

"Wyatt," Joe coughed, spitting blood into Wyatt's face, trying to shake him awake with one hand, whilst the other pressed into his chest, soaked in his and Molly's blood. "Wyatt," he croaked, shaking him again. Wyatt's eyes began to flicker open.

"Joe," Wyatt murmured, as he came to. "Joe?" Seeing the blood splattered on Joe's face, hands, and chest, Wyatt found himself waking up fast. But before Joe could reply, his eyelids winced, and his breath stuttered. He let go of Wyatt and fell. Wyatt struggled to his knees, reaching his arms out to Joe, and barely catching him, but he did, and lowered him down gently.

"Help," Joe's whisper was barely coherent, as he laid with his head back on Wyatt's knees, and his face between Wyatt's hands. Wyatt looked down, to see Joe caress the wounds in his chest, as he looked up at the ceiling.

"It's gon' be okay, Joe," Wyatt grimaced looking back into Joe's eyes, trying to wipe the blood from his face. A tear leaked from Wyatt, and onto Joe's face. Joe didn't feel it. His breathing was short, and he was staring into nothingness.

"I'm-," Joe stuttered spitting a little blood, "I'm a real cowboy," It was as if he were blind. Although Wyatt's face was directly above his, he looked right through it.

"Yeah," Wyatt whispered, knowing if he spoke too loud, his cry would become louder. Joe didn't respond, he just smiled through Wyatt, and tried to breathe.

"We need to go home now, Wyatt, it's gettin' late." A single tear trickled from the side of Joe's eye, sliding down his cheek.

"Come on, Joe," Wyatt panicked, more tears falling, as he shook his brother more frantically, trying to lift him but getting nowhere. *Momma's gon' kill me,* he thought irrationally, forgetting the place and time. "Joe!" Wyatt cried. Joe smiled, and his eyes slowly closed, "Joe! Joe! Time to go home!" Wyatt screamed, trying to wake him up, slapping his face and shaking his chest. He cried out, as he pulled Joe closer, and dropped down into his chest. He couldn't get in closer, his tears soaked into Joe's shirt and he couldn't let go. He raised up and began hitting into Joe's torso, "don't do this, Joe, it ain't funny no more!" Wyatt whimpered, staring into Joe's half-closed eyes, looking for life.

"Joe," he squeaked, flopping his head back down onto Joe's chest. Defeated, Wyatt held Joe's heavy, lifeless body into his own. The room was silent and empty once more, but continued to echo the sounds of death, with the muffled sounds of Wyatt's steady sobbing, desperately pressed into his brother's body.

He rocked, cradling Joe like a huge baby, crying relentlessly as he remained helpless, scared, shocked, and alone. The feelings of regret, failure, and grief grew stronger than ever.

I have failed you, Joe.

14: The Peak

The summit of Biting Rock, West California, April, 1880

"Puts things into perspective, doesn't it?" Carter stood ahead, one foot raised on a plinth, at the peak of Biting Rock, staring longingly at the town beneath and ahead. The journey was over, the morning reached an end as Wyatt limped and stumbled behind Billy following in Carter's wake. Wyatt's hands were tied, his head was drooping, his thoughts contemplating how much he took the horse's backside for granted.

The tall rocks and cliffs that once shaded the valleys and paths had dissipated, and the summit was vast and open, blasted by the midday sun, casting tiny shadows behind what little shrubbery there was.

"Faster," Carter turned back to call out to Wyatt, who still was struggling with the last inclined plane.

Wyatt coughed, and whilst choking blood onto the dirt, he tripped and fell. Without his hands to stop him, Wyatt smacked into the ground headfirst, puffing dust into the air around him as his feet kicked up behind him. Carter rolled his eyes and waved to Billy; "drag him," he said.

Billy thought about Al's fate, and how Carter had done nothing to help, he hastened Al's death. It filled him with sadness, he hadn't slept. How could you, next to your closest friend's cadaver? Instead, Billy had had all night to think about the look in Al's eyes in his last moments, and the smile on Carter's face as he pulled the trigger. Regretfully, he couldn't shake the feeling that Carter was right. Al had been done for, well that's what Carter said, and no one could have helped at the time. Reluctantly, he realised that Carter was his only friend, or at least acquaintance now. He walked to Wyatt's semi-conscious body, grabbed the back of his shirt, and began dragging him up the last few steps of the hill, like a corpse.

Wyatt was dropped at Carter's feet. "Wake up," Carter nudged him with a foot. As he opened his eyes, little drops of blood trickled from his eyelids and into his eyes, forcing him to blink it out. He couldn't move, his body had given up. The last twenty-four hours were a test for sure on his body, but despite his strength and endurance, it seemed as though his body had had enough. He laid motionless on the ground staring up at Carter's towering body.

So thirsty, he thought, attempting to communicate to Carter with only his face, and tongue.

"Cat got your tongue, boy?" Carter laughed, and gently placed a foot on Wyatt's chest, forcing a squirt of blood to spit from his mouth.

"Behold!" Carter looked ahead again, and rolled Wyatt's body with his foot to face the edge of the cliff.

Wyatt's pain shrunk, as he marveled at his home town at an angle, in all its glory. It was beautiful, even on its side. The delicate river could be seen all the way through the rows of buildings and beyond, flowing farther than the eye could see, surrounded by the red dirt paths and sparse plants that kept Rockriver healthy. And the tiny dots of people wandering and flickering in the sun; they made Rockriver home.

"Here we all stand, a perfect example of balance," announced Carter, removing his foot from Wyatt. Wyatt flopped onto his back and tried to force himself to roll the other way to face Carter, but the pain was stopping him. He had no choice but to stare up at the blinding sun.

"Sir?" Billy asked, baffled by Carter's introduction to one of his incoming lectures.

"Balance, Billy. Nature." Carter continued, "none of us belong up here with the snakes, but not all of us will die," he smiled. "Right, Wyatt?" he called out to Wyatt's body at the edge of the cliff. No response, just a strained huff. "Yeah, right," Carter nodded, agreeing on Wyatt's behalf and turning back to Billy.

"What you talkin' bout, s-sir?" Billy asked hesitantly, not knowing any politer words.

"God creates us with a fear of the unknown, yes?" Carter said as he began to pace, his hat in his hands. Billy shrugged, uninterested, yet falling short of a better idea than to listen.

Carter continued. "He does. For example, every man is born with a fear of snakes, and heights, and guns," Carter smiled, immersed in his own story, "yet here we stand, Billy, unafraid of those things, do you know why?" He approached Billy and awaited a response as he stared at him with a smirk.

"No," Billy said, looking goofy trying to mirror Carter's calm excitement.

"Because he also created *balance*," Carter grinned, and gestured to Wyatt's curled up body. "Despite these things we fear, he still will allow for the weak to make way for the strong." He laughed, and sauntered back to Wyatt, "hear me, boy?!" he yelled, trying to coax a response from Wyatt.

"K- k-," Wyatt choked. He couldn't talk, blood just spilled from his throat and stopped him when he tried. Carter knelt down and crouched to Wyatt's face, looking into his half-shut eyes, which flittered to Carter as he blocked the sun.

"Nothing to say?" Carter taunted, "well allow me to continue," he chuckled. "Now God can't control and balance everything, so he gave us free will. The reason we have free will, is so the strong stay strong," he patted Wyatt's face with his hat, "and the weak stay weak." He winked.

Wyatt couldn't talk, but spat upwards at Carter's face, pasting a small dollop of thick blood on his nose. Carter wiped his face down with the brim of his hat, and pursed his lips to spittle out any residue. He stayed where he was, disgusted but unmoved.

"Charmin'," Carter muttered, "would like to know your place in this world, as it comes to an end?" Carter leaned a little closer to Wyatt's still head. "Do tell me if you'd prefer for me to shut up." He waited for a response, and Wyatt opened his mouth, but still was held back by his wounds.

"Well alright," Carter smiled and stood. He looked out again over the town below. "I will say this one last time so you may take it to the grave; you are a *sinner*," he bellowed. He turned quickly, and swung his foot into Wyatt's ribs, cracking them as it landed. A breathy grunt came from Wyatt as he was crunched to the side. "You are a *sinner!*" Carter kicked him again, harder, cracking Wyatt's body further into a curved crippled shape. "*Sinner!*" one last boot, and he stopped. It allowed Wyatt to groan; at least it was a sound. Carter slowly dragged the toe of his boot on the dirt with a look of disgust on his face, smearing a short trail of Wyatt's blood on the ground, blending into the dry sandy mud.

"K- k-," Wyatt choked again, persistent, refusing to give up.

"As I said," Carter interrupted, pushing his hair back into place and settling his hat back onto his head, "God cannot control everything, so he must leave some things to the strong, and that is why he sent me."

Wyatt spat up a pained chuckle. It hurt his eyes, his ribs, and everywhere a limb joined to his body, but he refused to take Carter seriously.

"I am the righteous hand of God," Carter said with confidence, as he tightened his leather gloves before resting a hand on his holstered pistol, cocking the hammer.

"G- g-," Wyatt choked again, "give me a break," he said with barely a vocal cord. To Carter's shock, Wyatt was making noise. His hand lifted from his gun and he stomped to Wyatt's body.

"Think real careful, boy, or these words will be your last," Carter spat through his teeth as he quickly crouched to face Wyatt again.

"You ain't no righteous hand of God," Wyatt coughed up. Carter's eyes widened; he didn't imagine it. Wyatt spoke again.

"Enlighten me," Carter sneered down at him, "if your lungs don't give out first," he smiled.

"God-," Wyatt gargled through his blood-filled mouth, "God don't pull the trigger." Carter's breath sped up and his lips tightened. He was offended.

"Excuse me?" Carter whispered, struggling to maintain his authority, and fearsomeness, hiding his concern behind a feigned menacing brow.

"God woulda' let the snake do it," Wyatt choked and smiled through his red teeth, "You are the hand of the *Devil*," Wyatt coughed up a bloody chuckle, "Devil ain't afraid to pull the trigger."

His words hit Carter like a bullet and his lips trembled under his moustache. *The Devil?* he thought, transported back to his father's cruel words of satanic blame. *Was he right? Am I what the Devil left after he took Elmer Junior? Was father right about me?* Carter's eyelids flickered as he continued to stare at Wyatt, desperately trying not to overthink what Wyatt had said. *No.* He thought against Wyatt's mind games, *I am a good man.*

"Very well," Carter's confidence regained as he stood and smiled to Wyatt's surprise, "would you prefer I sit this one out?" Wyatt didn't respond, "Billy!" Carter shouted and stepped away.

Billy slowly walked closer, hunched and unsure, with his arms held inwards, rubbing his hands. "Sir?" he muttered.

"Beat this man," Carter ordered, and took a few steps away. As Billy approached Wyatt, he grew more uncomfortable, dragging his feet on the ground as Wyatt's bloody face became more visible. "Kick him!" Carter yelled as Billy stood over the body. Billy locked eyes with the blood already soaked into Wyatt's shredded clothes. Billy had learnt a whole new meaning of pain and death after watching it happen to his friend, and an unfamiliar feeling of sympathy started to set in.

"I'm sorry, Wyatt," Billy whispered, ensuring Carter could not hear. Wyatt's eyes drifted to meet Billy's above him.

"Kick him!" Carter screamed. Billy scrunched his face, and swung a leg into Wyatt's stomach, shooting Wyatt's eyes into the back of his head and jolting him sideways. "Again!" Carter yelled. Billy kicked again, sliding Wyatt across the dirt, closer to the edge of the cliff. "Again!" Carter ordered once more. Billy landed one last boot into Wyatt's torso, echoing the sound of another rib snapping like a tree branch.

Wyatt was crippled. His torso was misshapen and his limbs were lifeless. It was like only his eyes and mind were awake, and desperately looking for options. Carter fell silent, and walked back over to Wyatt and Billy, now that the beating had been served. They were at the edge of the cliff, toying with the chances of falling to their deaths.

Carter reached into his coat pocket to reveal a small fabric pouch and waved it above Wyatt's face.

"What's this?" Carter grinned, hanging the pouch above Wyatt's nose, "I'll tell you," he said as he pulled the string to open it, "*snake bait!*" he sneered as he emptied the contents onto Wyatt's chest. Crickets, frog legs, various tiny skins and bones, tiny creature's organs and what looked to be an assortment of herbs and spices. Billy watched as Carter threw the empty pouch off the cliff, staring at the contents garnished on Wyatt's body. *Strange,* Billy thought, racking his brain for the ability to put two and two together. "Want me to pull the trigger now?" Carter giggled and taunted at Wyatt, to no response.

Snake bait, Billy continued to mull over. His mouth was open when he thought, staring at various parts of the ground as his brain got to work. *Al? Snake bait?* It started to make sense, his heart began to race. "Snake bait?!" he shouted at Carter in rage. Carter was taken aback, offended by his inferior, and raised his eyebrow to question Billy's audacity.

"You speakin' without my sayin' so?" Carter asked, with an intimidating deep drawl.

"God damn snake bait?!" Billy yelled, breathing heavy, enraged. "You been carryin' snake bait all this time?!" His fists clenched as he stared at Carter's calm expression, "this was all a god damn game?! A god damn *lesson* or summit?!" he spat, and took a big step forward to Carter. He swung for him. He missed and tripped on Wyatt's body before falling beside him. Carter calmly stepped aside, closer to the cliff's edge, and faced Billy as he scrambled back to his feet.

Billy held up his fists ahead of him, and tried to breathe through his nose. He ran at Carter, with a fist cocked back and cried out a husky battle cry. Just as he approached and swung his hand, Carter dipped down and wrapped his arms around Billy's waist, barging his shoulder into his abdomen. Winded, Billy was lifted into the air as Carter stood, and hung like an angry toddler over his shoulder.

"Put me down!" Billy demanded as he thumped his fists into Carter's back. Carter stayed quiet, and solemnly took a couple of steps to the edge of the cliff and looked over. "No!" Billy whined, "Carter, no, it's me!" he continued to kick and punch aimlessly over Carter's shoulder, "I'm sorry! I'm s-…"

Carter hurled Billy off the edge of Biting Rock like a sack of sand. Billy's last words fell short as they developed into a scream, slowly getting quieter as he neared the ground. Thud, and the screaming stopped. The sound echoed up through the canyon, up to the summit, and into Wyatt and Carter's ears. The fluttering sounds of birds flying away from their disturbed peace accompanied the bleak sound of Billy's body meeting the dirt below.

"A necessary sacrifice," Carter said solemnly, "for man cannot thrive without the loss of others," he quoted a line of his own mantra.

The words brought Wyatt back to the man on his horse from the day before. The man who stopped in the badlands and looked out to them all as Wyatt received his first beating. The man Carter shot in cold blood. *The saviour,* as Wyatt recalled, the one who never got the chance to help. To Wyatt though, this memory brought hope; there was still a chance. One man in the desert meant that people pass through every now and then, maybe not as much as he'd like, but it happens. Even less often at the top of Biting Rock covered in snake bait, but again, his desperate mind grasped at the possibility.

"I've always admired your unwavering positivity," Carter interrupted Wyatt's thoughts, as if he were that easy to read, "it will serve you well in hell," Carter smiled.

"K-kill me, Devil," Wyatt struggled, daring Carter, whilst choking on his blood, his teeth wobbling in his mouth.

"I don't think I have to," Carter smiled back down at him, "and save the Devil's name for when he pulls the trigger."

Carter, having felt he'd finally found an ounce of peace, took a seat on the ground next to Wyatt's head and crossed his legs, whilst blocking the sun with his body. He looked out over Rockriver with Wyatt.

"At least you die with a view," Carter said calmly, "breathtaking." The sun beamed down on the town like a blessing from God, shimmering on the thin river that ran through the middle and over the horizon. Carter sat in silence for a little, hugging his knees and proudly looking upon Rockriver's dusty streets.

"I'd like you to know something," he said. There was no response from Wyatt, only strained wheezing as he continued to breathe. "Your wife told me where you were hiding."

Wyatt's wheezing stopped briefly, as his heart skipped a beat. "Liar," he winced and coughed.

"Not a liar, and that's not the only thing she gave me," Carter chuckled and waved his finger ahead of Wyatt, still staring at the land below. "She didn't even give it a second thought, couldn't wait to take the money," he continued. "You really hurt that poor girl, Wyatt," his tone became more serious, and he shook his head slightly.

He's toying with me again, Wyatt thought, *there's no way he really thinks I'll buy this bull.* Wyatt didn't want to talk, he just wanted it to be over. To him, it were as if Carter was just bored now, and sticking around trying to fill the silence until Wyatt either died or made a miraculous recovery.

"M- Mary loves me," Wyatt rasped, fighting the pain in his throat and chest so he could speak.

"Sure," Carter said sarcastically, "whatever you say," he pushed his fists into the ground and lifted himself back to his feet with a sigh. He looked down at Wyatt again and smiled at his bloodied and crippled, curled up body, positioned facing the town on his side.

A short silence filled the air's heat, gently echoing the community and distant civilisation of Rockriver, and Carter's hat once again shaded his face as he stared down.

"Well," Carter said jauntily, "I suppose it's true what they say; Biting Rock is a maddening place," and he began walking closer to his horse, readying her to leave. "I must say, Wyatt," he called out to Wyatt's still immobile body, "this journey has not been what I expected, if I'm honest, I brought you up here to kill you myself, but I believe this has been a little life-changing for me, spending all this time with you, wouldn't you agree?"

Wyatt tried to wiggle, trying desperately to shake the snake bait away from him before Carter left, but it was no use, he couldn't move. Carter jumped onto the horse and prepared to leave.

"I'll let God do my killin' now, like you said." Carter turned and began to canter away, back down the way they came up. Wyatt was left alone on the summit of Biting Rock, staring at his home. Immobile, struggling to breathe, unable to shift any of his weight, inches from the edge of the cliff, and within smelling distance of a lucky snake's favourite snacks...

15: Holier Than Thou

The Wilson homestead, West California, early April, 1880

Alone. Two months had passed since the beginning of Wyatt's journey to find Joe. Mary sat by herself, counting pennies on the table, waiting for Carter's imminent arrival for collection on Wyatt's debt. Falling a few weeks behind, she was once again thinking of a new excuse. *I was robbed,* she thought, *already used that. I lost it, no, not believable.* She scattered the pennies apart and began to arrange them. *$2.37, too short.* She spent hours a day searching for Carter's original stack of cash, praying that Wyatt had hidden it somewhere in the house, but knowing deep down it was likely on his person, or she'd have found it.

Her feathered hat sat dusty on the table. The reality of Wyatt's betrayal was bleaker than expected; it was uneventful and plain sad. She felt she'd betrayed herself, letting Wyatt leave thinking she'd have everything handled. But during his absence, Mary's situation was only exciting for a couple of days. She had thought that Wyatt would contact her and tell her when to run, or come back with Joe ready to burn the breeze, but he never arrived. Until, eventually she accepted it: she was going to be waiting much longer than expected.

Asshole, she thought as she finished counting and rested her head into her hand with an elbow on the table, gently rubbing her hairline in silent frustration.

She'd neglected the home. Dishes were in the sink unwashed, and dust was collecting on the floor and every surface. Most nights, she'd stare out a window at the path, hoping she'd see Wyatt and Banjo galloping towards her.

She couldn't sleep. The ceiling of the bedroom became a blank canvass for her to project and visualise her anxiety. *Is Wyatt okay? Is he coming back? Is he dead?* The scratches in the ceiling sometimes morphed into pictures and animations, of Wyatt fighting for his life, or Wyatt happier without her, or Wyatt with another woman. It was a difficult time; she was angry, scared, and alone, but she missed him, despite the deception, the lies, and the selfishness.

In her solitude, she had all the time in the world to theorise, but a conclusion never became clear. Perhaps he was scared to come back, or maybe he didn't want to come back at all, and planned to leave Mary alone.

A dirty smell seeped its way inside and caught Mary's attention. Not dirty like the unclean house, but more dirty like an animal. Faint murmuring came from the other side of the front door, whispering and tittering. Judging by the sun and how long Mary had been awake, it seemed around the right time for Carter to be back. *Has he brought a friend?* She wondered innocently.

"Mary?" Carter's voice called. The muffled second voice continued, incoherently.

"C-come in," Mary stuttered, startled by her own voice having not heard it for a couple of days.

"Mary," Carter smiled as he creaked the door open and appeared before her, "you couldn't make an effort?" he grinned, staring down at her messy hair, resting on the same dress she wore a week prior.

"There-," she lifted a finger with a quiver, "there was another-," she looked confused. *Another voice,* she thought, half asleep and tired, the words weren't coming out.

"Another voice?" Carter chuckled, "yes, come in," he said as he opened the door wider behind him.

Another man entered the room. *The smell!* Mary thought, *that's the smell!* Watching his boots, mud crumbled from them onto the floor with each step. His jeans were ripped in places and tiny flies hopped in and out of the holes. His shirt was baggy and filthy, shrouded by a rotten cloak. And his face was mean, scarred, and beaten. His chin was stained with dry blood, and through a sickening smile, his teeth were chipped and cracked.

"Allow me to introduce Mr Ellis Wood," Carter presented.

"A pleasure," Ellis gargled, filling his mouth with spit, visible through his crooked smile.

"Y- you're-," Mary's jaw shook, fascinated but terrified.

"I'm sure you've heard a lot about me," Ellis hissed, as Carter stood triumphantly next to him. Ellis approached the table slowly as Mary froze. She could swear that in the corner of her eye, tiny bugs were dropping from his boots with the dirt. His eyes stayed locked with Mary's terror as he crept closer, still holding that unsettling smile.

"A change of plan, Mary," Carter interrupted their staring and Mary's head flickered back to him, "chance and circumstance has brought myself and Mr Wood together." Mary looked back to Ellis to find his grinning face just inches from hers, staring, having her silently jolt in her chair in surprise.

"Ch- change of plan?" Mary tried to keep him talking, pulling her head back like a turtle, as Ellis was getting too close for comfort.

"Consider Mr Wood as an addition to our deal," Carter said, gesturing to him, "Mr Wood, if you will."

"Mary Wilson," Ellis drooled at Mary's face, "I have been looking for your husband and his brother," his grinned dropped, and blood rushed to his face, "for *four years!*" His face shook with anger.

"Calm down," Carter interrupted calmly. Like a dog, Ellis caught his breath and simmered down. He backed away from Mary's face and tried to compose himself, straightening his shirt as he looked at Carter, poorly emulating his professional manner. "Mr Wood found Wyatt's horse, wanderin' around outside of town - strange don't you think? Banjo is outside."

Banjo?! Mary worried, Wyatt was horseless, and still not back.

"I swore I would kill them boys," Ellis said, "and anyone who gives a ding 'bout them. That's you, princess," he sneered with an ugly grin.

"So, Mary," Carter continued, ignoring the fear in her expression, and Ellis's comment, "I must admit I have grown quite fond of you, so I'm going to miss you," he smiled. Mary was confused, *miss me? Is he going to kill me?* she thought in panic. Ellis slowly wandered around the back of Mary chair whilst Carter spoke. He was gently stroking her shoulders, lifting her hair and letting it drop back down, leaving Mary petrified in her seat trying not to shake.

"Don't kill me," Mary whimpered, still trying not to move while Ellis got far too comfortable with touching her.

"I won't kill you," Carter chuckled, "but he might," he gestured to Ellis, who while Carter looked at him, gave a curl of Mary's hair a gentle tug as he let out a heavy breath.

"What do you want this time?" Mary muttered, trying not to make any sudden movements with her lips or body with Ellis in her personal space.

"I want to find Wyatt," Carter said sternly, "now that I don't have to keep an eye on you." He began checking his nails and took his eyes off Mary, letting Ellis briefly take the spotlight. One unattended smile from Ellis, foretold a threatening future for Mary.

"I don't know where he is, I told you," Mary said quietly, breaking the silence. Carter laughed under his breath.

"Mary," he chuckled, "lying is not so *holy* of you." He wandered a little closer to the table that Mary was counting change on. With a sudden switch of his demeanour, he slammed his fist on the table, bouncing the change an inch with a jingle, "I have been *patient!*" he yelled, as a drop of blood came from his knuckle. He marched to Mary and lowered himself to her face, pointing a bloodied finger at her eyes, "now, Mary, Mr Wood is *not* the soft touch that I am!"

"I'm not," Ellis whispered to himself with a smirk, as he circled the two of them.

"Last chance, Mary," Carter continued pointing. His face was rarely so angry, but it frightened her so close. *Stay strong,* she thought.

"I-, I don't know," she squeaked, trying to back away from his finger, calling his bluff and trying to stay strong. Carter huffed and lowered his finger. He stood up again and turned away to pace a little.

"Why do you do this, Mary?" he said angrily and frustrated trying to stop his hands from waving by stuffing them in his coat pockets. "He *left* you! Betrayed you! Why do you protect him?!" he yelled.

He wouldn't, he's coming back, Mary thought, refusing the respond, still uncomfortable with Ellis's creepy movements around the room, and still wary of Carter's anger and frustration.

With agitation and a sigh, Carter pushed his hand inside his coat and revealed a large wad of dollar notes. He slammed them on the table next to Mary and crouched down again.

"Name your price," Carter said, breathing heavily through his nose as he stared.

"There's no price," Mary replied, "I'll never tell."

"So, you do know," Carter said quietly to her after a brief silence, letting out a smirk, "and everyone has a price."

"Not me," she stood her ground, but was internally frantic after slipping up.

"I don't think you understand," Carter continued to sneer, "once I leave you with Mr Wood, don't you want a head start?"

"On what?" Mary asked, intrigued through terror, behind a mask of feigned confidence. The confidence wasn't working.

"Didn't you hear me?" Carter belittled her, "he's not the soft touch that I am," he began to poke her chest as he spoke, "tell me where your traitor husband is, take the money, and run before I leave, because once I leave, you're in Ellis's hands," he smiled with a furrowed brow. Ellis stood still behind him, smiling, and eagerly waiting for his turn alone with Mary, to chase for sport.

Could she? The money was on the table, and it had been weeks since she'd been alone. A new thought wheedled its way into her brain: *Wyatt deserved this, he left for his own interests, really.* Deep down, perhaps he never cared what she thought, or what would happen to her. She knew she didn't have particularly long to think about it, making the decision all the more difficult. *No,* the thought entered her mind as if it were intrusive to her. *Go, run,* the next thought was almost more appealing. She couldn't guarantee what would happen if she stayed or ran. *Would Wyatt die? Come back? Would Ellis kill me?* One thing was for certain; if she took the money and ran, she'd be alive at least a little longer. A blessing in her current circumstances.

All of this could be over so soon, she turned over in her mind in the silence. *Wyatt might not even still be at the brewery, it's been weeks,* she justified internally, clearly, the money would help her, and she could stop worrying. *Banjo is just outside,* she thought, *where is Wyatt?* A man's horse wandering alone is never a good sign, but perhaps Wyatt was just hiding, and Banjo was a liability. *Hell,* she thought, *take it and run, I'll find Wyatt after I kill Ellis Wood.*

"I want it all," Mary whispered catching Carter's attention, as she looked at the floor.

"Atta girl," Carter smiled, and pulled up Wyatt's empty seat next to Mary…

16: Draw

The abandoned Carter & Smith Brewery, California, one day before the events of Biting Rock, April, 1880

With Billy and Al behind him, Carter was armed with guns, ropes, and a bag for Wyatt's head, all packaged onto a horse's rear. It was early morning, and although there were birds singing from the thicket of brush around the abandoned building, each man's stomach was filled with anticipation and tension. Copying their melody, Carter softly whistled along with the birds. They approached Carter's father's old brewery building gently trotting on their individual horses, with the fresh knowledge of Wyatt's last known location, courtesy of Mary.

About twenty feet from the front door, Carter noticed two rectangle patches in the dirt, like the ground had been disturbed and placed back down. He stopped whistling, and brought all three horses to a stop with a quick raise of his hand. There was a slap-dash, make-shift crucifix jammed in the ground next to the disturbed dirt, made of small bunches of twigs and sticks, tied together with bloodied rope.

Carter stopped and stared, momentarily unsettled.

"Dig," Carter ordered, prompting Al and Billy to dismount. They knelt down at the patches, looked at one another, shrugged, and began pushing their fingers into the dirt to dig, whilst Carter watched down on them from horseback.

Al's fingertips brushed something more solid than mud, and he slowed his scrabbling, gently brushing the soil, and gradually unveiling something in the dirt, just inches below the ground's natural surface.

"Mr Carter, look," he shuddered, swiping the dirt away from a blackened, burnt face below him. Grimacing, Al turned away, and swallowed the bile rising in his throat. Carter hopped down to the ground and crouched cautiously, gently pushing Al aside.

"God damn," Carter whispered in awe, brushing the dirt aside by his own hand, showing a loose, burnt piece of fabric with a floral pattern. Carter's brow furrowed, and ragged thoughts gathered at the edge of his consciousness. *Could it be...?* His mind tried to push the realization away, but the dreadful recognition could not be denied as Carter placed the fabric next to the body's charred and squashed, almost unrecognizable face. Almost unrecognizable. *No!* screamed Carter's mind, but the cold rage had already begun to surge. *Molly...*

"Who is it, Mr Carter?" Billy asked from behind. Carter didn't move. He couldn't- wouldn't- say it aloud, weakened by reality and denying the truth. His lip quivered, hidden by his moustache, but invisible to the others anyway, and he remained, head tilted towards the ground.

Refusing to respond, he gently brushed the dirt back over the top of his sister's burnt face and body, then stood and glared at the second grave, not caring for the identity of who might be inside it.

Stepping away from the shallow graves, his breathing grew heavy as he looked back up at his father's old, abandoned brewery. He left the horses and stormed towards Al and Billy. He held his hand out to Billy, and snatched a pistol from his belt, before heading towards the building, stomping his feet with purpose and unholstering his own gun with his free hand as he walked. Al and Billy looked on, then turned to look at each other, silently questioning whether to follow him.

The door was a tad open, with the broken padlock on the ground. Pushing it ajar with the butt of a gun, the memories flooded back. All of the anger and resentment from his past, met with the newfound grief and hatred, and combined to form the sweat that dripped down his creased, enraged face as he looked around the remains of his unhappy childhood.

"Wyatt?!" Carter bellowed through the building, gripping both pistols tightly at his sides. A faint flicker of candlelight emanated from a dusty window in the corner of the vast emptiness, illuminating Elmer Senior's old office, where Henry had spent his early years. Skeptical, and uncomfortable with his whereabouts, Carter took tentative steps towards his father's office. His boots gently tapped the dirty floor as he walked, echoing softly. Dotted sparsely, old and dusty units of heavy machinery remained abandoned too, rusting as time elapsed. *Lots of places to hide,* Carter thought, trying to peek behind each machine he passed, cautiously wondering if the candlelight in the office was just a diversion, and if Wyatt might be expecting him.

The candlelight persisted, but the door was closed, and the window was too dusty for Carter to see inside. *Ironic,* he thought as he drifted back in time, *a window for Father to watch his workers, but always too dirty to see shit.* Yet another reason to resent his father.

Finally, standing outside the office, he saw no signs of movement inside. His breathing quickened, but he fought the fear, reassuring himself internally, *Wyatt can't shoot no more,* but his environment pressured him. The discomfort of being back in the brewery triggered an irrational fear and tension and he looked down at his feet and tried again to become his more composed self. *I'm not scared,* he repeated to himself, trying to rationalise his intrusive thoughts.

Pointing the barrel of one pistol to the door and gently pressing it into the wood, he slowly creaked it open, swearing he could feel the heat from the candle creeping through the opening.

Within, sat Wyatt, cross-legged on the floor, staring down. He appeared deflated, resting his hand on an open page of a book. He didn't even look up, but Carter could see that his hair was scruffy, his hands were filthy, and scattered around him were the remains of burnt-out matches. *He must have utilised the remaining contents of the room,* thought Carter. The drawers on Elmer's old desk were opened and empty, and hollow tin cans and glass bottles were stacked lazily in the corner.

Sensing a presence, Wyatt lifted his heavy head to face Carter in the doorframe. To Carter's delight and disappointment, Wyatt's face was stained and shiny from copious tears, his eyelids hung low and darkened, deprived of sleep and sunlight.

"You dare rob my father?" Carter gritted his teeth and uttered quietly under the gentle flickering sound the candle emitted, being met with the vacant gaze of Wyatt's run-down mood.

"Carter," Wyatt wheezed, in the voice of a man who had not spoken in weeks.

"That's mine," Carter whispered, pointing a barrel down at Wyatt's feet, where his hand held a bible open on the floor.

"You read it wrong," Wyatt muttered under his dead eyes, referencing certain sentences of the bible that a young Henry had shakily underlined in pencil.

"Last chance," Carter said, throwing one of the pistols on the floor at Wyatt's feet. It clanged as it landed, and slid with a scrape, "be grateful for my mercy." He turned back around and left the room, dragging his feet back to the open plan factory floor, where Al and Billy waited like a small audience, having caught up with Carter, but stood hesitant to interfere.

Wyatt accepted his truth, that Carter was always eventually going to catch up. All the time wasted worrying about whether to return to Rockriver or to run further; weeks stuck between the hammer and the anvil. He flopped the bible closed, and reached for the gun before him. *There is no point running from this,* he thought, unready to face the fight before him, but unwilling to die without his pride.

His legs felt weak, but with a wobbly effort, Wyatt rose to his feet, the pistol in his hand. He looked down the barrel and into the chambers, counting just two bullets.

The pistol hung from his finger loosely, and he waddled after Carter with his arms flopping by his sides. Carter waited, in the dead centre of the abandoned floor, hovering his hand above his holstered weapon. He watched as Wyatt slumped out of the office door, gently tapping his foot with impatience.

"I expected more from you," Carter muttered, but his voice carried through the silence of the building, as Wyatt wandered closer to face him. As he approached Carter's face, their eyes lined up, and Carter tried to maintain his formidability and authority, despite being unsettled by Wyatt's defeated and apathetic gaze. It was almost as if Wyatt feared nothing, having already lost everything, but his face was much too impassive for Carter to read it.

"Are we doing this?" Wyatt mumbled, as he faced his opponent from just a foot away. He holstered the loaned gun to mirror Carter, and waited for a response whilst trying to maintain his poker-face, as this was the only form of intimidation he had left.

"Billy!" Carter shouted to the side, "begin." Billy wandered to meet them in the middle of the room, and in his goofy, shaky drawl, he spoke with permission.

"Gentlemen," where Billy stood, he created a small triangle between the three, with Carter and Wyatt staring into each other's eyes, not blinking, "turn to have your backs to one another," Billy ordered. Carter and Wyatt kept their gaze while they rotated slowly, until they broke their stare and stood defenceless, reluctantly trusting the other not to turn back around and attack prematurely, "I will count to twelve," Billy continued, "you each take one step away from each other every time I say a number, got it?"

"Understood," Carter said.

"Just start," Wyatt said at the same time as Carter, neither of them being entirely coherent over one another.

"I ain't gon' kill you yet, Wyatt," Carter muttered behind Wyatt.

"You should," Wyatt retorted under his breath.

"Where's the fun in that? You need to feel pain first," Carter responded. Although not being able to see his face, Wyatt could tell there was a smirk behind his comment, and feared for what Carter might be planning.

"One," Billy said, breaking the whispers. Both men took a step forward and away from one another, listening carefully for the echoes of the other's footsteps, to ensure no cheating was involved. "Two," Billy continued, feeling the tension rise as Carter and Wyatt grew more skeptical of one another. Every time the number rose, they stepped closer to the inevitable gunshots, or to possible betrayal.

He could spin around any second and shoot me in the back, both Carter and Wyatt thought in unison, listening to Billy's slow, steady counting.

"Three."

And hearing each other's rhythmic footsteps get gradually and steadily more distant.

"Four."

What if I miss? Wyatt thought, *will I be the one to shoot first, or should I wait for him to shoot first? I only have two bullets.*

"Five."

He will surely miss, Carter thought, knowing there is always a possibility that Wyatt will break the rules, and *what if he doesn't miss?*

"Six."

Halfway, they both thought. As Billy's counting neared closer to twelve, he began to shuffle backwards himself, cautious of being caught in a crossfire. Al, almost invisible to the other men in the room, watched frightened from a distance, but ready to jump forward and into action if Carter so desired.

"Seven," Billy's voice was getting quieter to Carter and Wyatt, but only echoed louder. Their own footsteps over his voice were becoming more prominent to themselves.

Wyatt peeked his eyes gently to his side upon his seventh step, trying not to make it obvious, keeping his head forward to not arouse suspicion. To his right, was a short row of three empty barrels, standing upright next to each other, presumably abandoned along with the brewery. The thought of shooting early was more desirable now, *I can take cover if I miss,* he mulled over, weakened by the knowledge of his own poor accuracy.

"Eight."

Wyatt looked forward, there was nowhere else to hide past these barrels.

"Nine."

To hell with it, he thought. Wyatt spun quickly and drew the gun from his belt. Before Billy or Al could warn Carter, Wyatt had already pulled the trigger, shattering the silence with a crushing bang and its echo, like thunder and lightning had struck straight through the ceiling. Carter flinched and ducked in the distance, and saw Wyatt dive behind the barrels as he turned back around.

"Coward!" Carter screamed through the gunshot's echo.

In a panic, Wyatt held the pistol to his torso as he sat and wriggled behind the barrels, frantically looking around to find a way out, having already wasted one of two bullets with a poor, impulsive, blind decision. *Shit, shit, shit,* he panicked, hearing the sound of Carter's boots getting nearer.

There! He looked ahead in his only field of vision. Behind a large glass cutting machine in the corner, another door was obscured by dust, decay and low light, with the exception of the outdoors shining through the dust in the door's tiny window. *If I can just make it there,* he thought, considering it to be just one frantic crawl away.

"Coward!" Carter screamed even louder as he stomped closer to Wyatt. Feeling the oncoming danger, Wyatt sprung his body upwards and twisted to point the gun in Carter's direction. He fired his only remaining bullet in a cold sweat. In fear, he realised that it had sped past the top of Carter's shoulder and pinged against a metal girder on the ceiling, a tinny sound piercing through everyone's ears. He ducked back down immediately having seen Carter raise his arm ahead. Multiple loud bangs from Carter's pistol penetrated the barrels at Wyatt's back with deafening thuds, each one making him shudder and flinch as Carter emptied the chambers of his pistol, in time with his steps marching forward.

Now, Wyatt dropped the gun by his side, took a deep breath, and scrambled for the back door. Carter's shooting ended, as he pulled the trigger one last time to be met with the simple click of an empty weapon. He slammed the gun to the ground and began to run after Wyatt, seeing him crawling on his belly for the door.

"You yellow-bellied piece of *shit*," Carter spat as he stopped Wyatt in his tracks, violently grabbing both of his legs and pulling him backwards. Scraping his nails into the floor, Wyatt grasped at its rough surface as his legs were akimbo and he slid further away from the exit.

Carter flung him back down, bouncing Wyatt against the barrels and onto his back. Mercilessly, and without allowing Wyatt a chance at composure, Carter threw his fist down, and collided with Wyatt's nose, cracking it as the blow landed.

Wyatt's head slammed against the ground, and everything became a haze. He could see the wobbling silhouette of Carter above him, stepping away, and could hear the muffled voices of Al and Billy approaching.

He begged his eyes not to roll back and close, but the effort to avoid it made his vision less focused. And in those moments, he saw a silhouette again reach down to his face with what looked like a bag. And then it was lights out.

17: Dust To Dust

The summit of Biting Rock, West California, April, 1880

This wasn't supposed to happen.

And back to basics. Wyatt laid on his side facing the town below, with a gentle evening breeze massaging his bruised, sunburnt, cut-up skin. Right where Carter left him, too weak to escape the peak of Biting Rock.

This isn't how it was supposed to end.

Wyatt did not fear death. In his experience, it looked peaceful, and whatever followed would have to be more enjoyable than the societal fallout of the last decade.

No, Wyatt feared the loss of his memory. Afraid that once the lights go out, the memories go with it. Would they follow him to the afterlife? Although trusting in his faith, the question was always there.

All this life, what with its causing problems, and its chasing dreams, and its getting past the challenges that preface them, maybe Wyatt wouldn't even make it to heaven, and maybe Joe never made it either. Of all times, this was surely a time to believe, because what is there to lose?

Son of a bitch, he cursed as he stared down over the edge of the cliff, watching the distant dot that was Carter, walking his horse back across the plains, returning to Rockriver. Although, this time, the curse was not only for Carter. Wyatt felt as though he failed, and instinctively blamed himself too. There was no way to feel righteous or strong, as the light wind blew dust and flies into his eyeballs, whilst he tried desperately to keep them open.

It stung, of course, the flies and dust. The dust like the tiny needles of the reaper, trying to force him to close his eyes and die. The flies, bouncing around his face, trying to find the first patch of dead skin to begin their feast. It was irritating, but even if he had the strength, he wouldn't waste his energy trying to swat them away. Every ounce of life he had left, was dedicated to savouring every last moment, and he intended to make the flies wait their turn.

Will I die before or after the snakes find this? he wondered, rolling his eyes down to his belly, where Carter's bait laid next to him, *God, I hope so,* he rolled his eyes back to the town, uncomfortable with wishing his own life away, but terrified of his other possible fate, after seeing with his own eyes the kind of horror these snakes can inflict on a man. On the other hand, he was in some ways grateful for being alone, should the snakes be his fate. No one should have to see that. *Maybe this bait is fake anyway,* he thought, confused by the mere idea of so-called 'snake bait.'

Wyatt's mouth was wide open, with his cheek pressed against the dirt. He felt a metallic, wet tang drip down from a loose tooth in the back of his jaw. *Blood,* he thought. In the dire heat, it dripped on his dried-out tongue and moistened it for a brief, beautiful second of momentary relief. He wanted to lift his tongue to the bleeding tooth, to coax out a little more, but instead, waited for it to drip again, thinking if he forced it, then the relief wouldn't feel as good.

Don't get distracted, focus on the town, he repeated inside, hoping visual concentration would keep him awake. Just then, a distance away on a church steeple in Rockriver, a minuscule gliding dot landed, accompanied by the quiet, unmistakable screech of a vulture. *This asshole,* he thought, thinking back to his encounter with Ellis Wood and the tribe in Texas, the vulture being his friendly, bleak reminder of how realistically short a distance he had come, and how easy it was for this creature to find him. Despite its distance, Wyatt felt the same bittersweet sensation of the vulture watching him, just as he felt before.

A drop of blood dripped again from his tooth and onto his tongue, once more adding another tiny sting of life to his failing, drying body. *Relief,* he thought, as a shudder of satisfaction sparked through his body. It shortly faded, and he focused again on the town, waiting for the next drop.

I wonder if she is still there? He looked longingly homeward, thinking fondly of Mary, and denying Carter's previous comments. *She will be fine,* he thought. Whether Carter was telling the truth or not, Wyatt knew somehow that Mary would be okay in the long run at least. She had always hidden it from Wyatt, but he often had a strong feeling that she was much more capable of looking after herself than she let on. She often seemed bored of her wifely duties of late, which indicated to Wyatt that there was something she was missing about life before they met. But he never thought to ask about her past, it was always conversations about Joe, and his mother, and Texas, and himself.

In his solitude, he finally felt regret for his selfishness, realising too late that his hubris and only thinking inwards had ultimately been his undoing. The thoughts of 'if only I had listened to Mary', 'I should have thought of Mary', and 'I should have just left it alone', bounced around his unravelling mind.

He thought, or rather, prayed, that Mary was alive and okay. If not, however, he planned to make amends in the afterlife. Carter may have just been playing a game, but he had a point, Wyatt had hurt Mary. Whether it was for recent actions, or just the slow steady build of resentment. If she had in fact betrayed him, Wyatt was just grateful she hadn't done it sooner, she must have truly loved him despite his consistent duplicity and disloyalty.

Another drop of blood blessed his tongue. It felt like a reward for his self-reflection, like God trying to subtly say 'correct, well done, Wyatt.' Wanting to reward himself further, he debated the idea again of using a morsel of energy to wiggle more blood from behind his tooth with his tongue. *If I don't get it now, I might die before it stops dripping,* he thought, justifying his desperation.

It hurt, but he slowly lifted his tongue to his bleeding tooth, guilty of the kind of impulsive, greedy, and impatient behaviour that he knew Mary hated. As it made contact, the sour taste of his blood touched his tongue, but with a gentle touch, his tooth dropped from its socket, tumbled out of his mouth, and onto the ground in front of his face. The tooth's absence allowed the blood to drip freely, and more frequently. He rested his tongue back down and allowed for the blood to drip onto it, each time further covering a larger surface of his tongue.

The sky turned a pale red, as the sun took its first dip into the horizon. With his eyes only partially open, Wyatt's vision was a little blurry, and the light from the sun's rays appeared as long golden spikes, blessing everything they touched.

Evening sunlight hit the ground in prongs, like many hands on a clock face. It was too bright to determine whether Wyatt was really seeing it like this. Nevertheless, he was in no state to debate reality.

His eyelids flickered, trying to stay open, but trying not to be blinded as he stared directly at the sun without a choice. Thinking it will be fine once the sun fully disappears. He couldn't focus entirely, but it almost looked as though the prongs of light were shaped into the outlines of a person. Two prongs hitting the ground, and two either side. *Who is that?* Wyatt thought, as this strange sunlight figure became more and more person-shaped as his vision blurred, and he struggled to focus through the irritating little dots that the sun had pasted over his retinas. *That is a person!* Wyatt thought, as it looked like the sunlight figure had a hat and a cloak, also twinkling in sunbeams.

The sunbeams appeared again more sparsely, and another figure appeared, and another. Three sunlight beings were before Wyatt. But he was facing the sun on a cliff edge. Were these figures flying? Or right in front of his face and tiny? The wind began to pick up, just as the figures looked like they were moving, staring at Wyatt. The sun disappeared a little more, and the top of Biting Rock was a little less bright. The figures were no longer beams of sunlight. They were darker, like shadows flickering in between day and night at sunset.

The wind brushed over Wyatt's ear sounding like a faint whisper. It was like the three figures were discussing him between each other, and communicating using the wind. The whispers came from all directions, and he couldn't determine whether these sounds were actually coming from these beings in the sky.

Take him now, Wyatt heard, he swore he heard it, in the whispers. *No, wake him up,* another whisper tickled his ear.

They are real! Wyatt thought, with sudden realisation, desperately trying to move. *The dark watchers. Joe was right. I can't wait to tell him.*

As the figures ahead of Wyatt floated, he thought back to Joe's story at the campfire. The dark watchers appear before those who are about to die, or before somebody close to you dies. *Surely, he wasn't right,* Wyatt thought, reluctant to acknowledge what could have just been an exhausted daydream.

It's too late to change, Wyatt, he heard echoing in the wind again, as the sun disappeared a little more. *The voices are right,* Wyatt thought, pretending it wasn't just his guilty conscience.

I am changed, please have mercy, Wyatt thought he said, but he didn't actually feel his mouth move, and he didn't feel the pain of moving. He was sure he heard himself speak though. Or maybe it too was just the wind.

We are not who you must ask for mercy, the beings replied together, whispering like the breeze, *ask the right person for mercy.*

They're right, Wyatt thought, remembering Joe never actually said they had anything to do with death and the afterlife, only that these beings would be present. *So, I must ask God?* Wyatt thought again, but heard his own voice echoing like the dark watchers.

Perhaps, the watchers replied with a hiss. A hiss that was closer to his face than the dark watchers seemed.

The watchers resumed with incoherent whispers blending with the various sounds of dust and breeze. Wyatt couldn't tell what they were saying, and he couldn't concentrate well enough to listen. It was like he was falling asleep and the sounds around him were blending too well. Their whispers had a touch of hoarseness. Like a hiss, mixed with a rattle.

A rattle?! Wyatt sprung back awake. The dark watchers vanished into nothingness, the sky was clear, and Wyatt's eyes opened wide. He heard a light rattle, and felt his feet gently touched as something slithered past them, disturbing the ground as it got closer to the bait in front of him.

Stay still, he thought in panic, as if he had any choice. He peeked down to his belly, and saw a small rattlesnake testing the air with its tongue near the bait Carter left, just inches away. The snake peeked up, and locked eyes with Wyatt. It wasn't startled, it was fine with Wyatt being there. It almost looked sympathetic to him, with its eyes looking somewhat gentle and empathetic.

Why isn't it killing me? he thought, confused by the snake's unsettling gaze. *Maybe it doesn't have to.*

He looked away from the snake and to the town again, when another drop of blood came from his tooth hole, like the view of the town had become a reflex after he got a taste of blood. *I'll ask the dark watchers what they think,* he thought, but they weren't there anymore. It was just sky and the distant town again, but darker, and cooling down a bit.

This is reality, he squeezed out a little sigh, disappointed by the watchers' departure. But their whispers still rang true, if they were real; he didn't want to let this snake kill him, or simply die before he'd asked the right person for forgiveness.

The snake slowly wriggled up to Wyatt's face, and continued to stare, having a better look. As they looked at one another, Wyatt felt its eyes looking deeper than just his face, like it was trying to understand why Wyatt was there, and what the story could have been. The strangest part being that it looked like it knew everything already.

Wyatt felt connected, like Joe at the stream drinking with the doe. It was a good feeling, at peace as the world around him took his life back. It was not Wyatt's world, he had just been borrowing it, from the snake, from the deer, from Joe, and from Mary.

Accepting, he mustered every last ounce of his energy, and tried to move his hand closer to the snake, feeling the urge to further connect with it in his last moments. *First this snake will forgive me, and then I will beg for more,* he thought, as his whole body ached with the tiny, strained movements in his arm and hand. The snake wiggled a little, and raised its head, looking down on Wyatt's moving hand, agitated by the disturbance.

Wyatt closed his eyes, preparing for the intense pain that may follow, and not wanting to see it. Little by little, his hand reached further out, waiting for the harsh, real pain of the snake's teeth, or for the icy grip of the reaper's hand.

His mind focused on the watchers' words. *Ask the right person for mercy,* he thought, *okay.*

> *Holy Mary, Mother of God, pray for us sinners, now and at the hour of our death. Amen.*

No noise came from the snake as his hand got closer. But in what felt like Wyatt's final moments, the unmistakable, distant sound of somebody's footsteps echoed elsewhere on the peak of Biting Rock…

To be continued.